BULLET FOR A STAR

BULLET FOR A STAR

STUART M. KAMINKSY

MYSTERIOUSPRESS.COM

Cover design by Jim Tierney

ISBN 978-1-4532-3680-2

This edition published in 2013 by MysteriousPress.com/Open Road Integrated Media
345 Hudson Street
New York, NY 10014
www.mysteriouspress.com
www.openroadmedia.com

For Merle

BULLET FOR A STAR

1

IT WAS THE SUMMER OF 1940, a hot August day in the San Fernando Valley, and I had doubts that my '34 Buick would even get to Warner Brothers. The pistons were making threatening noises, and with four bucks in my wallet and nothing in the bank, I tried to ignore the sound. I was, I hoped, on the way to a job.

I totaled my assets and salable qualities as I turned down Barham. I was on my own, had my office rent paid till the end of the month, knew a dozen people I could hit for a few dollars, including an ex-wife who worked for an airline and liked me but long ago gave up loving me—with good reason. My health, except for an occasional sore back, was good, though it wouldn't be much longer if I had to keep living on nickel tacos and cokes.

My face was in my favor. I badly needed a haircut, but sometimes the slightly wild look was just what a client wanted in a bodyguard. My nose had been broken at least three times, once by a baseball thrown by my brother, once by a windshield and once by a fist thrown by my brother, in that order. But at five foot nine, the nose was a valuable asset. It announced that I had known violence.

I had been about to answer an ad in the L.A. Times for a part-time commissioned skip tracer for an auto agency in Fresno when the call had come from Sidney Adelman at Warner Brothers. Sid said he had a job for me if I could get to the studio in a hurry. I didn't bother to ask what the job was. He knew I didn't care. I survived a shave with a thrice-used Gillette Blue Blade and put on my only decent suit and unwrinkled tie, being careful to knot it over a small egg stain.

Four years earlier I had been fired as a Warner Brothers security officer. I'd made the mistake of breaking the arm of a Western star who had made the mistake of thinking he was as tough in person as he was on the screen of Grauman's or Loew's State. The broken arm had caused a two-week delay on the star's latest classic. The order to fire me had come directly from Jack Warner.

For the past four years I had barely survived as a private investigator. The jobs had been few: helping a house detective named Flack in a second-rate hotel during conventions, searching for missing wives of shoe salesmen, picking up days here and there as a bodyguard for movie stars at premieres. I had Mickey Rooney twice, and he was hard to keep up with; but MGM didn't argue about the salary and paid it fast.

I pulled up at the Warner gate behind a black Pontiac. The uniformed guard at the gate, a big-bellied, good-natured giant named Hatch, motioned Walter Brennan through, and I eased forward. As I reached through the window to shake Hatch's massive, hairy right hand, I wondered why the studio had suddenly forgiven me.

"Toby Peters, for Chrissake. How you doing?"

Hatch was about 60, but his grip was inescapable. There was a car behind me, a limousine with a chauffeur waiting to go through the gate.

"I'm making it, Hatch, and they tell me times are getting better."

"God willing," he said, "but that European war don't look good."

I nodded.

"Hatch, Adelman sent for me."

"Right, he called down. You know where the building is. Take Litvak's space. He's on location somewhere."

I thanked Hatch and drove through slowly past two of the block-long, barracks-like Warner buildings and a flock of extras dressed as pirates. Eventually, I slipped down a narrow alley to the office building where Sid Adelman hung his nerves.

Warner is a labyrinth of two-story rectangular buildings, outdoor sets and sound stages. Adelman's office was on the first floor of one of the office buildings. Sid was called a producer, but he didn't produce many things that made their way to the screens of theaters. He had started by getting coffee for the Brothers Warner when they were still junk dealers. Now he listened to the woes of studio stars, sympathized with directors' complaints, delivered ultimatums, arranged parties, kept secrets and made lots of money. He was only fifty, but looked sixty.

The long corridor was busy with hurrying people. Girls with long skirts and porcelain faces trying to look like Wildroot Cream Oil ads, men with cigars who wanted to be recognized as producers, guys with their collars open, whose weary smiles announced that they were writers and had nothing to do with the others in the hall.

Sid's office was where it had been four years before when I had last been in it. I had done a few odd jobs for him, like carrying drunks from parties, muscling a persistent fired cameraman who claimed the studio owed him a year's salary, and keeping my mouth shut about a very important female star who had a session with drugs and a friendship with a married senator.

Sid's outer office was the same as I had remembered it. The walls were covered with autographed, framed photos, all studio publicity shots, of Warner stars. The only thing that had changed in the office was the girl sitting behind the desk reading a Street and Smith love magazine.

"What happened to Louise?" I asked affably.

"Did you wish to see Mr. Adelman?" she answered unaffably, looking up from her reading. Her face was like those in the hall, pretty, ready to crack and young/old. Her hair, over her painted eyebrows, was a lacquered, brittle tower of dark yellow. I wondered how she could sleep without breaking it and decided from the blank look on her face that it was probably her biggest worry.

"My name's Peters. He called me."

"Have a seat," she said, returning to her magazine. "Mr. Adelman is in Viewing Room Three and will be back in half an hour."

Normally, I would have sat down humbly, but she annoyed me by being stupid, which I wasn't, and having a job, which I didn't.

"I'll join him," I said, heading for the door.

"He wanted you to wait," she said in exasperation at having to look up again.

"That's O.K., Maisie. I know the way."

"My name's not Maisie. It's Esther." I closed the door.

I walked back down the hall, spotted Jack Norton, the guy who always played a drunk, and made my way back into the California sun. I was starting to sweat. I sweat easily, and with only three shirts I couldn't afford it.

As I crossed the fifty yards to the screening room, I almost bumped into a kid who made me feel a little better. He was carrying two huge cans of 35mm film and was sweating even more than I was.

Screening Room Three was one of five in a lifeless, one-story rectangle. The screening rooms offered different sizes and levels of plushness. Number Three was the simplest, with thirty seats arranged like a theater. I opened the outer door and stepped past the small projection booth, where I could see an old, hard-of-hearing studio projectionist named Robby leaning back in a chair and doing a crossword puzzle. Whatever he was screening didn't interest him.

I opened the inner door to the theater and stood still, waiting for my eyes to adjust to the darkness. The first thing I saw was the image on the screen, a black and white, silent film. A tall, skinny, good-looking boy on the screen was standing bare chested in a forest arguing with a girl who came up to his waist.

Only two other people were in the screening room, sitting in the middle row. One was Sid Adelman. The other seemed to be a youngish man with Harold Lloyd glasses. Harold Lloyd leaned close to catch any great words that Sid might drop.

"What's the kid's name?" Sid grunted in a put-upon New York accent.

"Bradley," said the young man.

"No, schmuck, not the kid who made it. The actor. That big kid." Sid pointed to the screen, his hand breaking the projector beam and crossing over the young actor's face.

"Uh," said the young man flipping through some notes and turning them toward the screen to catch enough light to read them. "Heston, Charlton Heston. He's 17 and . . ."

"Jesus," groaned Sid. "I wonder who made that name up."

I shuffled my feet as noisily as I could on the carpet, and the two men turned toward me. Adelman stood up, so Harold Lloyd stood up.

"Peters?" Adelman asked.

"Right."

"All right. All right," Adelman shouted. "Turn it off." Nothing happened. "That deaf son-of-a-bitch. Robby," he shrieked, "turn that fucking thing off." Sid was one of a townful of Hollywood characters who swore two decades before it became generally popular.

The projector went off with a whine and the lights went on.

"Some kids in Ohio," Adelman said, shaking his head toward the screen.

"Illinois," corrected the young man at his side.

"What's the difference," sighed Adelman. "These kids made that picture, a full-length version, silent of some Russian or Greek play, *Peer Gynt*. Who wants it?"

Sid looked at me. I looked at him. As bad as I looked, he looked worse. At least I hoped so. Even with his elevator shoes, Sid Adelman topped no more than five foot four. His hair was dirty grey and as thick as style would allow, to give him another fraction of an inch on the world. The bags under his eyes were permanent, dark heavy, packed and ready to go for more than twenty years. The light brown suit fit perfectly around his stomach, but the shoulders were too wide. Throwing in the suit, elevator shoes, haircut and paunch, he weighed no more than 120 pounds.

The young man stood beside Adelman, waiting. If he straightened up, he would have been a good four inches taller than his boss. And if he took off the glasses, he would have been a good looking man, but he wasn't about to straighten up or take off his glasses with Sid around. He reeked of brains and ambition.

Sid came out of the aisle and took my arm, pulling me down a little toward him.

"I've got a job for you," he stage whispered, ushering me through the doors and back into the sunlight.

"Cunningham, go write a letter to those guys," he barked over his shoulder.

Young Cunningham nodded efficiently and hurried away without a glance at me. Cunningham, a damn good yes man, would go far at the studio. Sid was now dragging my left shoulder dangerously close to the ground.

"The things these actors get into," he whispered, "you remember." He paused to put on a gigantic fake smile for a fat, well-dressed man well up in his sixties, who passed by us, a cigar in his mouth as big as Sid.

"Looking good, Morris."

Morris nodded, preoccupied.

"An asshole," confided Adelman, guiding me into his office building. "A producer with three straight shit bombs." He smiled and shook his head in mock sympathy.

We passed an open office door, and I could see Jack Benny sitting in a chair and looking up with full attention to a minute, ancient woman in black who was shouting, "Every time, every time."

Esther lifted her heavy head as we entered but didn't bother to put away her magazine.

"Mr. Peters and I are not to be disturbed," Sid told her, guiding me into his office and closing the door.

His office was large, with a big window looking directly at another huge window about ten yards away in a similar building.

There was a man in the other window. He wore a dark sweater, had a mustache and unruly hair and held a pipe in one hand as he looked up in the sky.

"That," said Adelman pointing directly at the man, "is Faulkner, the writer."

Adelman looked at Faulkner, who smiled genially and went back to looking at the sky. Sid shot me a look to see if I knew who Faulkner was. I didn't bite, and he continued:

"You know what he's costing us for two weeks' work? MGM didn't want him, and you know what we're paying him?"

"No," I said sitting across the desk from Adelman, who had not offered me a seat.

"Don't ask," he said, tearing his eyes away from the writer and sitting uncomfortably in his chair, an oversize leather monster.

The office was remarkably plain for a producer: dark carpeting, a big desk, a bookcase full of scripts, and two pictures on the wall, one of the Brothers Warner and one of President Roosevelt. Both were autographed. A small refrigerator stood in one corner, and there were two plain chairs for visitors.

"Well," beamed Sid, turning from studio hen to salesman, "How have you been? Can I get you a drink?"

"No drink, thanks. I've been doing fine."

He shoved a couple of pens and pencils into a desk drawer and looked over at me.

"You've been doing lousy," he said evenly.

"I've been doing lousy," I agreed, "and I'd like a beer."

He got up and hustled to the refrigerator. He talked as he moved and brought me a bottle of Ballantine's beer with a glass. The glass had a decal of Porky Pig on it.

"You know, Peters, I had nothing to do with your getting booted two years ago. I want you to know that."

"It's four years, Sid, and I never blamed you."

I poured the beer slowly and watched Porky's eyes turn amber from the liquid. Faulkner smiled across at me and turned away.

"You know," Sid went on, after looking at me intently while I took a long drink, as if I hadn't a care in the world, "you had one quality I always admired."

"My rotten temper. But I'm older now." I tried to make it sound wise and ironic.

"No, no, no," he said. "You're honest. You keep things to yourself. You saw something here and you kept your mouth shut even when you got axed. You follow me?"

"You've got a secret for me to keep."

"In a way. In a way." He took the pens and pencils out of the drawer he had just put them in and arranged them on his desk. He was silent for about thirty seconds, looking at his pencil and pen arrangement. I drank my beer and looked at Bill Faulkner's back. I felt like he and I were old friends, and things were finally going our way.

"Blackmail," Adelman finally spat out. The pens and pencils went back in the drawer. "One of our stars is being blackmailed."

"And?"

"What do you mean, 'and'? And I've got to take care of it," he said, looking at the photo of his employers on the wall.

I finished my beer.

"We . . . I've decided to pay them," Adelman said, reaching into the drawer again and pulling out a thick envelope. "There are five thousand dollars in one hundred dollar bills in here. I want you to deliver them to a certain address at two in the morning. We don't want any studio people involved, and we don't want anyone to know anything before or after. You give me your word that if anything goes wrong in the transaction, you don't involve me, the studio or the actor."

"What do I get in exchange for the envelope?"

"A negative and a positive print," said Adelman softly. "You don't give up the money until you have the negative and print. Then you bring them back to me."

I shook my head.

"They can have a hundred copies of that picture, a dozen negatives," I said. "The five thousand is just a down payment."

"You think I'm some kind of putz off the street," Adelman said, rubbing his forehead and standing. "Our actor says the picture's a fake. Maybe it is; maybe it isn't. We have a man who can tell if he sees the original negative."

"And if it's real?" I asked with a slight grin.

"We'll handle it."

"You mean pay some more, find someone nastier than me to handle it, or dump the actor?"

"That's our business," said Adelman, turning in his chair where he was again sitting.

"Where's the print the blackmailers sent your actor?"

"I destroyed it immediately," Adelman barked. "I didn't want someone else to get it and make more copies."

"All right," I said standing. "Answer three questions, and you have a delivery man."

"Good," Adelman sighed, turning to face me. "The answer to your first question is $200 now and the same when you hand me the negative and print. Now your second question."

"My second and third," I said holding up two fingers. "What's in the picture, and who's the actor? I'm going to know both answers when I make the trade, and you want to be sure I know what I'm dealing for."

The little man hesitated, touched his hair to be sure it was still there and threw up his hands.

"It's a picture of a man and a girl, a very, very young girl." He handed me the envelope and counted $200 from his own wallet. I took the cash and pocketed it.

"You make the exchange at this address in Los Angeles," he whispered. "You take the envelope there at two in the morning." He scribbled on a sheet of paper and handed it to me. It was a middle class area off Figueroa near the University of Southern California. "You go to the door, make the exchange and that's all."

"You checked the house?" I asked.

"It's empty, for sale."

"O.K.," I said, thinking that I had plenty of time to fix my piston, get a reasonable meal, listen to the radio and get some sleep before the delivery. "Now for the other question I asked."

Adelman nodded and moved to the door. I caught him glancing at the portrait of the Warner boys and followed him out and past Esther the reader. This time he didn't take my arm. I caught up with him as he burst through the door of the building. Wet patches of sweat immediately wilted his collar.

We cut through a sound stage where the cast and crew of what looked like a football movie were taking a break. Pat O'Brien, wearing a Notre Dame sweatshirt and a baseball cap, was telling a joke in a heavy, put-on Irish accent. He paused to wave at Sid, who dashed through a door and hurried to another building.

The halls of this small building were empty. I knew the building and the name on the door where Sid stopped, looked up at me, raised an eyebrow and knocked. A male voice answered cheerfully, "Come right in. It's never locked."

We stepped into a combination dressing room and den and were greeted by the lone occupant, who advanced on us. He was a tall man, easily six foot two, wearing a Union cavalry uniform and carrying a drink of clear liquid in his left hand.

"Sidney," he said with genuine affection, "always good to see you."

Sid glumly shook the extended hand of the man towering over him. The man turned to me with a warm smile, a touch of curiosity and familiar, even, white teeth. He shook my hand firmly and appeared every bit as confident and likable as he did in his movies.

"This is Toby Peters," said Sid, collapsing into a chair. "He's going to make that transaction for us. Toby, Errol Flynn."

2

"MR. PETERS," FLYNN BEGAN, guiding me to a soft brown sofa, "may I call you Toby?"

"Sure," I said, taking a seat. He sat next to me.

"A rather minor character in my first picture at this studio . . ." Flynn began.

"*The Case of the Curious Bride,*" Adelman's voice rose wearily from the chair in which he was slumped but couldn't be seen, "and you were a rather minor character in it."

"True," continued Flynn with a grin. "This minor character, at a crucial moment in the plot, shouted, 'this is a frame up.' Please imagine, Toby, that I am shouting those words. Mind you, I am not above the sort of thing implied in the photograph. As a matter of fact, I strongly advocate it, but it is illegal."

"And very bad publicity," came the voice of Adelman. I looked at Flynn, who sighed, took a drink of the clear liquid and added, "quite right."

"I am not a citizen," he continued, "and it would be a rather simple matter to ask me to leave the country, which would displease me, the studio and, I modestly hope, a great many moviegoers. Can I get you a drink? Vodka?" He held up his glass. I said no, and he went on.

"My past is not entirely *sans* blemish or incident. When I was a boy in Australia, I ran with a gang of razor robbers, cutthroats. When they murdered a friend, I headed for New Guinea to seek my fortune. Instead I spent some time in jail for assaulting an unsavory Chinese and, a short time later, was within inches of losing my life, when I was put on trial for killing a headhunter who had attacked me."

It was fascinating, but I wondered why he was telling me all this.

"I'm telling you all this," he answered, reading my mind, "because I want you to know that if I did spend some time with the young lady . . ."

"Very young lady," came Adelman's voice.

"All right," Flynn smiled, lifting his hands in mock defeat, "very young lady, I would gallantly admit it. I have known very young ladies both in and out of the jungle, and I do not forget any of them. I have never seen the young lady in that photograph I saw this afternoon. However, Sidney has convinced me that, under the circumstances, we should pay."

There was a shuffle in Sidney's chair, and he rose to his full five feet and a few inches as he faced us sourly.

"And the circumstances," he said, "include the fact that you are in the middle of some very delicate divorce proceedings."

Flynn rose, put his drink down and looked at his face in a mirror on the wall. Then he looked at my reflection over his shoulder looking at him.

"You know," he said turning to me, "a few weeks ago I was a pirate. Today I'm in the middle of a Western. This business can be very confusing." He walked over to me, and I stood up. He put an arm around my shoulder.

"Toby," he said softly, "I am thirty years old and getting very wealthy. I am a product, a voice, a face, a body. I make three or four pictures a year to get as much out of that product as possible before it wears out. What I would dearly like to do is take your place for that assignation and break the blackmailer's goddamn neck, but I'm too big an investment."

He guided me toward the door, and Sid walked after us shaking his head.

"Why don't I forget the money and issue a challenge to the guy to meet you in Griffith Park with swords at dawn," I grunted.

It wasn't much of a joke, but Flynn leaned back in his blue uniform, teeth showing, hands on hips, just like in *The Adventures of Robin Hood,* and laughed loudly. It got me. For a second I was a ten year old at a matinee instead of a shabby, part-time bodyguard in his forties with a mashed nose.

"I like you, Toby," said Flynn shaking my hand again, "and I trust you."

"I'll do what has to be done, Mr. Flynn," I said, and I meant it.

"Call me Errol or Princey."

Sid and I went into the hall.

"Princey?" I asked looking at Sid.

Adelman shrugged. "He picked it up from *The Prince and the Pauper.* He likes it, and he wasn't even the fucking prince."

"I'll be in my office all night. You call me as soon as you have the negative and the picture and bring them here immediately."

"Right," I said looking at a well-built redhead who hurried by, in bizarre costume, reading a script.

Adelman went back to his office, and I retrieved my Buick from Anatole Litvak's parking space. The piston sounded worse as I backed out. My mind was racing ahead, and I almost hit the redhead. Big feathers drapped over her behind bounced as she jumped out of the way and screamed at me.

"Jerk, you almost killed me," she shouted. I turned to apologize, but she had already turned away.

I drove through the gate, waving at Hatch.

"Good to see you again, Toby," he called, lifting his ham hand and flashing oversize teeth.

"My best to Jack Warner," I shouted back.

I drove past the golf course across from Warners, where Jack Warner, Sid Adelman and half of the talent at the studio weren't permitted because they were Jewish.

It was four in the afternoon. I dropped my car off in a garage near my apartment on Eleventh Street, gave Arnie, the no-necked mechanic eight bucks in advance and told him I'd be back in two hours. He smiled around a stubby cigar, and I went home and changed clothes.

Twenty minutes later I was at the Y on Hope Street where I paid the last three bucks on my year's membership and spent fifteen minutes on the track and ten on the small punching bag. Then I got up a handball game with a lean banker named Dana Hodgdon. He was 62 and beat hell out of me every time we played.

By eight I had my car and ate my first steak in months at Levy's Grill, downtown on Sprina. Carmen the cashier, a dark and recent widow, gave me a smile when I paid. Everyone was smiling at me. I felt great and invited her to a late movie. Her wide mouth over her ample everything asked for a raincheck, and I said O.K.

I went back to my apartment, turned on the fan, listened to Gracie Allen tell George Burns about her brother for half an hour, and set the alarm. I stretched out on my unmade bed and dreamed I was Robin Hood. I swung on a chandelier, waving a sword, and speared a photograph out of Basil Rathbone's hand. I turned my back and was about to get clubbed by a combination of Claude Rains and Sid Adelman when Alan Hale saved my life. I looked down at the photograph and saw that it was me in a compromising position with Carmen the cashier. She was wearing a child's dress. I woke up. The alarm was ringing.

I put on my pants, shirt and holster, complete with 38 automatic. In the ten years I had owned the gun, I had never fired it at anyone or wanted to. I seldom loaded it. Some clients expected a private investigator to have a gun and felt disappointed if they didn't spot one under his jacket. This time I loaded the gun. I didn't expect trouble. The only thing I had that the blackmailers wanted was an envelope of money, and I fully intended to give it to them. But you never knew what a nervous or stupid criminal might do. Sid Adelman was paying me $400 to be less nervous and a little smarter than the blackmailer.

The streets were almost deserted. They usually are in Los Angeles. Thousands of people move to the city every week, but it has a lot of space to fill. I went down University and headed toward Figueroa. I pulled up in front of the address Sid had given me. It was one of a series of spread out, not very big one-story bungalows with small front yards. It was two minutes to two. I checked my flashlight and envelope and let the inside of my arm touch the firmness of my holster through my jacket. It was reassuring.

There was a "For Sale" sign on the lawn, just barely visible by the street light. The house was dark and silent. All the houses on both sides of the street were dark and silent. I knocked gently. Nothing. I knocked again and this time heard someone move quickly across the room behind the door. The door opened suddenly and a beam of light hit me in the face. I flashed my light back on a dark hood with two round eyes.

The hooded being, dressed entirely in black, held a gun in one hand and an envelope in the other.

"Nice night," I said, reaching slowly in my pocket for the envelope of money. I wanted to hear his voice. He was about my height, maybe a little taller, and not as broad in the shoulders. He said nothing. I shrugged, pulling out the envelope. "Just trying to ease the tension."

He carefully took my thick envelope and handed me his thin one. I opened his, put the flashlight under my arm and looked at the photograph and negative. It was Flynn's face. The girl was on her stomach. He was behind and on top of her. They were both baby naked, and she was looking directly at the camera with a dreamy, distant smile. She looked even younger than I expected, and I could see why Sid was nervous.

The black hood shuffled. He looked up at me with sudden fear in his eyes and began to raise his gun toward me.

"Now wait a minute," I said, taking a step backward. With that step I realized the fear wasn't directed at me, but the person whose foot I stepped on. Before I could turn, I was pushed forward into the hooded man. We fell in darkness and something hit the back of my head. I tried to hang on to consciousness and the photograph, but both were going fast.

There was a distant tug at the picture in my hand. I pulled back, but something hit me again, and I started to go out. From far away I thought I heard a shot. Alan Hale, I thought, where are you now that I need you?

I opened my eyes to almost total darkness. I didn't know if I were lying or sitting and didn't much care. The hell with it. Existing was getting damn difficult. I tried to move and felt as if someone had punished me for the effort by driving a rusty spike between my eyes. I could taste the spike. My hand shot up to my head and came back wet with my own blood. My only decent suit and shirt were a mess.

I figured out that the floor was under my chest. I pushed, but fell over, a balloon swelling in my head. Sitting up was the hardest thing I had done since I told my old man I was quitting college. I tried to think, but someone was groaning so loud and breathing so heavily that I couldn't. I knew the groaning breather was me.

My eyes slowly focused for the dim light from the street, and I crawled in the direction where I thought my flashlight had flown. It took me about three weeks to find the flashlight with every effort expanding the balloon in my head. I started to groan again but realized there was no one to feel sorry for me. The flashlight was still working. The beam had no trouble finding the hooded corpse in the middle of the room.

I reached for my gun. It was gone. My watch said 2:05. A lot had happened in five minutes. My best bet would be to get the hell out of there, but my legs told me it would be slow going. I crawled to the body. He was in a fetal position. I was sure he was dead even before I turned him over and saw that someone had dotted his right eye with a bullet. I pulled the hood off. His eyes were open, and he looked frightened and surprised.

So was I. The man was Cunningham, Sid Adelman's assistant,

minus his Harold Lloyd glasses and his life. I was a lousy judge of character. He would never make it in the Warner organization.

Somewhere inside my painful head I knew that the little hole in Cunningham's head was made by my 38. His gun was still in his hand. I smelled it. It hadn't been fired. The shot had made noise, and there was a better than even bet that the L.A. police would be coming through the door any second.

I wiped blood from my eyes and searched the body and around it. No identification. No money. No negative. No photograph. I looked down at my red hand and realized that my fist was closed and I was holding something.

Toby, I told myself, be a good guy and open your hand. Let's see what you've got.

It took a few seconds for the request to make it from my brain to the hand, but it opened, and I looked down at the face and vacant eyes of the girl in the picture. I had held on to it when I was hit, and the corner with her face had come off in my hand. I stuffed the fragment of photograph in my pocket and tried to stand. The door was kicked open. If the killer had come back to finish me, he was going to have no trouble.

Light hit me in the face, and I winced with pain.

"Don't move mister," said a young voice.

"I can't move," I tried to say, but it must have come out sounding like a ten-month old eating cereal.

Another beam of light searched the room, and I tilted my light up. There were two young Los Angeles cops with flashlights and guns. Their dark ties were neat, and their shields gleamed over their left pockets.

"I think this one's dead," said the young-voiced cop.

"And I think this one's drunk," said the other one helping me up. He was big and had no trouble lifting me with one arm. "He's hurt too."

His hand touched my holster. He reached under my jacket to check.

"You've got troubles mister," he whispered almost sympathetically.

You don't know half of it, I thought.

ONE HOUR LATER, after a quick trip to Los Angeles County General Hospital where a nervous medical student sewed up my head, I was feeling again. Not really better, but feeling and starting to think. I was sitting with the big cop in a police station, a wide, dirty room. The smell of stale tobacco and human sweat hung over the few desks. An ancient NRA eagle poster peeled off of one dirty wall. The cop looked at me with curiosity and took off his hat to rub his head. For a young man, he had very little hair.

I said I was sorry for getting blood on his uniform, and he said it was all right.

A coffee cup was hot in my hand. I sipped, but each sip hurt. Everything hurt.

"The sergeant says you can make one call before he talks to you, but we've got to listen to what you say."

"Shouldn't you be out in your car or on your beat?" I asked.

"We're short-handed, vacations. You kill that guy?"

"No. You believe me?"

He shrugged.

Adelman was waiting for my call and a negative, but I had promised to cover for him, the studio and Flynn. I'd screwed everything else up. At least I could do that.

"No call," I said. "Just get in touch with Lieutenant Pevsner in Homicide. Tell him I'm here and what happened."

"You want Pevsner?" said the young man, unable to believe the request.

"Yes, please."

"Your funeral," he shrugged again, "but I'm not calling him. The sergeant will have to do it."

A few minutes after four I was feeling almost alive again. The big cop had moved with me to Pevsner's small office. There was barely enough room for the battered desk, a steel file cabinet, two chairs, him and me.

Pevsner came in, looked at me and then at the big cop, who put his hat back on and started to turn on his friendly smile but thought better of it and left. He did the right thing. Pevsner slammed the door and moved behind the desk glaring at me, a manila folder in his hand.

He was a little taller than me, a little broader, a little older and developing a slight cop's gut. He had close-cut steely hair and the look of a lunatic who required superhuman effort to hold in his rage. The last time I had seen that look was when I went with him to the Louis-Roper fight in Wrigley Field a year earlier. Joe Louis had kayoed Jack Roper in the first. Phil Pevsner had felt cheated and angry. His tie was dangling loosely around his neck.

"You look like a pile of crap," Pevsner said.

"How are Ruth and the kids?"

"You have a phone in that tin office of yours," he said. "You know my number. This is no goddamn time to ask me about my family. Did you shoot that guy?"

"No."

"Where's your gun?"

"I don't know."

"What were you doing in that house, and how did you get your head bashed?" He looked up from the report in front of him.

"I got a call early in the evening," I said trying to sound sincere. "Some guy said he had a job for me, guard for some truckers' union official who was getting threats. The guy said the union man was hiding at the house, and I should come there at two in the morning."

"Why two in the morning?"

"I don't know," I said wearily. "Maybe someone was following him."

"So?"

"So, I went to the house at two. Someone opened the door and used my head for batting practice."

"You see anyone?"

"Too dark."

"You know the guy who was killed?"

"No."

"Toby," Pevsner sighed and pursed his lips, "You are one shitty liar. Who are you covering for?"

"Errol Flynn," I said.

Pevsner stood up in a rage, his hands going red and then white as they clasped the edge of the desk.

"Cut that wise-ass crap, Toby, or you're going to catch a phone book in the face."

I put my two hands up, palms toward him. I knew from experience that he meant it.

"Phil, I've had enough for one night. I know you can give me more. I didn't kill that guy."

"Shit," Pevsner answered, throwing the folder on the desk.

"Did you find my gun?"

No answer.

"Come on, Phil. What did I do, shoot that guy, bury my gun, beat myself over the back of the head and sit around waiting for the cops?"

"Toby, I know when you're lying. Your story is full of holes, and the holes are plugged with horse shit."

"Are you going to book me, Phil?"

"Not yet. Get the hell out of here. When I find out who that dead man is, we're going to have another talk."

I left him sitting behind the desk with his back to me. The big cop who had brought me in was waiting in the hallway. I winked at him and made it down the steps and into the night air.

Phil Pevsner didn't always like me, and he wasn't always honest; but he believed me when I said I hadn't killed Cunningham. Pevsner was a good, tough cop, and I didn't think it would take him too long to find out the dead man was a Warner Brothers employee named Cunningham.

The big cop had driven me here in my own car which was parked in front of the station. There was a parking ticket on the windshield, but I still felt lucky. I'd probably have been locked up listening to drunks if my brother Phil weren't a homicide cop.

3

BY THE TIME I HAD SHOWERED, changed into my last suit, had a bitter cup of coffee and finished a bowl of Shredded Wheat with sugar and milk, I was ready for Sid Adelman.

"Peters, you know what time it is?" his voice cracked.

I looked at my watch, tucked the phone under my chin and poured myself another cup of Chase and Sanborn.

"It's a quarter to five. Do you want to hear what I have to say or do you want me to listen to you complain?"

"Talk," hissed Adelman.

"I've been in the hospital and a police station." Adelman groaned, and I continued. "Don't worry. I kept you, Flynn and the studio out of it. The blackmailer's dead."

"You killed him?"

"I didn't kill anybody. Somebody killed him, cracked me in the head and took the cash, the negative and the picture. But I don't think you'll hear anything more about the photographs or blackmail. There's a murder rap tied to the pictures now. He'll probably burn them faster than you would."

It sounded reasonable, and I hoped Sid would buy it.

"This is . . ." Sid began, but I heard a scrambling and someone took the phone from him. Then I heard Flynn's voice.

"Toby, are you all right?"

"A few stitches, a bloody shirt, but I'm all right."

"Good man. I should have come with you."

"Just for the record, Errol," I said, sounding as buddy-buddy as I could, "were you and Sid together at two?"

"Why yes, did you suspect us of something?" He sounded delighted with the idea.

"Not really, I just wanted to be sure. Do you know Cunningham?"

"Cunningham?" Flynn repeated.

"What about Cunningham?" Sid's voice came in. He had obviously picked up the phone in his outer office.

"He was your blackmailer. He's dead."

"You're drunk."

"I don't drink."

"Sid," Flynn's voice broke in calmly. "Please be quiet and let Toby talk."

"Thanks. I need Cunningham's address," I continued. "The cops don't have any identification on him. Maybe I can get to his place and find something before the law does."

"Like more prints or negatives," said Flynn.

"I'm looking," sighed Sid. "What a goddamn crazy business this has turned into. You give a young man a break . . . Here it is, Charles Henry Cunningham, 1720 Montana, Santa Monica."

"O.K., Sid. If the police contact you, don't tell them about the blackmail and don't mention me. Meanwhile, make up a list of anyone who could have known the address where the blackmail exchange was made. I'll get there as soon as I can."

"We'll have it ready," said Flynn resolutely. "I've got to be on Stage Five for a montage sequence in an hour. Sid will come with me. Meet us there. And let me know if there's anything else I can do to help."

"Thanks, Errol, I will. Sid, when did you hire Cunningham, and where did he come from?"

"Christ, I don't know. I hired him a couple of months ago. Somebody recommended him."

"Who?"

"Who? I don't remember."

"Try to remember. It may be important."

I hung up and headed for Santa Monica as the sun came up over the mountains.

The Montana Avenue address was a fake adobe, one-story courtyard building with palm trees, a dozen apartments and a swimming pool the size of a bathtub. Cunningham's apartment was easy to find. His name was on the door. I knocked. A gun would have been comforting, but the only one I owned was the missing 38.

The apartment was silent. I tried the door. It was locked. I pulled at the window and it gave a little. With a sharp push, I snapped the tiny hook that held the window. I stood still in the courtyard for a second or two to see if someone had heard the noise, but all was quiet. Stepping through the window, I pulled the drapes fully closed behind me and turned on the wall light.

The room was neat, like a hotel room the maid has just visited. Either someone came in daily to clean it or Cunningham had been a very dainty housekeeper. Searching was easy. There was one small bedroom, a smaller kitchen and a living room. The furniture was typical furnished apartment, once colorful, now fading. There was a camera and tripod in a closet and enough equipment to convert the bathroom into a makeshift darkroom. There were no photographs or negatives of Flynn and the girl, but there was a small photo in a dresser drawer. It showed Cunningham and a woman. They were on a beach, probably not far from this apartment. Cunningham and the woman were in bathing suits. He was waving at the camera making his left hand blur slightly. His right hand and arm held the woman. She was an extremely well endowed blonde with short, curly hair. She was wearing dark glasses and a sour expression and didn't seem at all happy about having her picture taken. She looked vaguely familiar.

I took the photograph and added it to the one in my pocket, the head of the young girl. As I left through the front door, a woman came out of the next apartment. I turned my back to her and stuck my head back into Cunningham's apartment.

"Is a no problem, Chuck," I said raising my voice a few octaves in my best Chico Marx accent. "I'll picka them up later." The woman's steps clicked past, and I withdrew my head.

The sun was out, and I was feeling unreasonably good. It was idiotic. My gun was missing; I was a murder suspect; I had fouled up a job and had my brains scrambled, but I felt cunning and powerful.

Back at the Warners' gate, Hatch stuck his head into my car to greet me.

"What happened to your head?" he gasped.

"Twelve stitches," I said.

"I'm really sorry, Toby," he said, and I believed him. I was certainly a sorry sight.

"Hatch, I'm supposed to meet Errol Flynn and Sid Adelman on Stage Five."

"Sure, Toby, go on in. You know the way."

"Thanks, Hatch."

In the rear-view mirror I could see Hatch's hulking form aimed sadly in my direction for a second or two before turning to an arriving Cadillac.

Stage Five was where all the montage and special effects were shot at Warners. A paternal ex-cameraman from the silent days, named Byron "Bun" Haskin, ran the place like a separate kingdom. Montage, which the studio used a lot, was a series of short shots to show the passing of time in feature films. Maybe ten or fifteen shots of Wall Street crumbling and men taking dives out of windows with ticker tape in their hands, or eight shots of Jimmy Cagney walking up to doors that shut on him. That was montage. Big directors didn't shoot that stuff, or inserts, shots of hands or objects. All that was done on Stage Five.

I found Sid Adelman on Stage Five sitting in a director's chair almost asleep with his hands folded on his stomach. On the western saloon set in front of him, Flynn was solemnly throwing punches at a camera and missing it by inches. He was dressed in cowboy clothes and a broad, white hat. There were five people on the set. The montage director, a kid with curly, dark hair, a thin mustache and a worldly voice, called:

"Perfect, Errol. Let's have the lights and take that."

The lights went on. The cameraman took a reading. Flynn adjusted his hat. The cameraman crouched behind the big Mitchell camera, and the young director called "Roll and . . . action."

Flynn punched viciously at the camera.

"Good," said the director, "just keep it rolling. Try a couple more punches, Errol." Flynn dutifully punched as the young man instructed.

"Cut," called the director. "Thank you, Errol, looks fine."

"Thank you, Donald," Flynn said, spotting me and walking in my direction. "Toby, old man." His hand went out to me. Flynn was about ten feet from me when the first shot pinged off the light near his head.

Nobody on the set paid particular attention to the sound, but I recognized it, and, apparently, so did Flynn. I dropped to the ground and shouted:

"Everybody down, get down. Somebody's shooting."

Adelman jolted awake and went comically on his hands and knees. The young director went flat, and his crew joined him.

Flynn neither went down nor looked for cover. From behind a prop box where I had rolled, I could see Flynn standing bolt upright and glaring angrily. The second shot hit somewhere near his feet.

"For God's sake, Errol," I shouted, "get behind something. He's shooting at you."

Near the darkness of the door I had come through a few minutes before, a figure moved. The door opened and closed. Flynn, his cowboy hat flying off, ran for the door. I got up and ran after him. My idea was to try to keep him from getting a bullet up his perfect nose, but he was moving fast and got to the door before me. I ran to his side and looked out. There was no one in sight.

"Cowardly bastard," Flynn mumbled. "My life is a charade. I don't even have a real gun to defend myself with." He held up his studio six-shooter and shook his head, a wry smile on his lips.

We went back inside Stage Five, and I did not mention the likelihood of the recent shots being from my gun.

Adelman was shaking. The young director called out:

"Everybody all right? Equipment all right?"

"Maybe we better call the police," Adelman whispered.

"What do you think, Toby?" asked Flynn.

"Errol, I think you should suddenly get sick for a few days and go to a hotel where no one can find you. Can you cover for him, Sid?"

A pale Adelman said yes.

"Now wait a minute," Flynn said.

"Look," I countered, sitting heavily in a chair on the saloon set while Flynn retrieved his fallen hat, "I admire your courage, but it's not needed right now. I don't know what's happening, but I'd like to have a few days to work on it. Someone's trying to kill you and drop Cunningham's murder in my lap."

"Toby," said Flynn, clasping my shoulder, "I don't like hiding."

"Errol, it will keep you alive. Did you make that list for me, the list of people who knew the address where I went this morning?"

Adelman fished through his pockets and came up with a crumpled sheet of paper. There were three names on it.

"Sid, I and those three were having lunch together when the envelope arrived," Flynn explained. "We had no idea what it was all about at first, and by the time it dawned on us, everyone at the table had seen the picture and the note with the address and meeting time. They all promised to forget it and Sid destroyed the picture."

The list of names was:

DONALD SIEGEL

HARRY BEAUMONT

PETER LORRE

"O.K. Errol, now please go find a hotel for two days. Don't tell anyone where you are. No one, not me, not Sid, not your best friend. Call Sid this afternoon and tomorrow afternoon. He'll keep you informed. I know you don't like it, but believe me, it's the right thing."

"All right. I believe you," he said, touching his fingers to his forehead in a gesture of farewell. The opportunity for a dramatic exit probably turned the trick. "I'll get in my car at once and go out the back gate."

When Flynn left, I turned to Adelman.

"Sid, I have about $175 left from what you gave me. That should be enough, but . . ."

"Not another penny until you deliver the negative and print," he said, "or proof that they are destroyed." Scared to death and confused, he did not forget a $200 business deal.

"All right. I want to get started on this list right away. Who is this first guy, Siegel?"

Sid told me he was a kid in his twenties who had a reputation for montage and was getting into second unit directing.

"What's the kid like?"

Sid shrugged. "Cocky. Too much confidence, too many practical jokes, but sharp."

"Where do I find him?"

"That's him." He pointed at the young man who had just directed Flynn's punching bit.

"Did you remember who recommended Cunningham to you?"

He didn't, but said he would keep thinking. As he walked away, I turned to find Siegel. He was no longer in sight. I went into the darkness behind the saloon set and found the cameraman examining the camera for bullet holes. He said his name was Bob Burks and that Siegel was in the next building. I thanked him and found my way through a door and into the next building, a huge sound stage set up to look like a gymnasium, complete with bleachers.

There were only two people on the set. They were in a far corner playing ping pong. One of the people was Siegel wearing a blue tee shirt. The clopping of the ball echoed through the building.

As I approached I could see that he held his tongue in the corner of his mouth and was concentrating on playing. The other man, who looked like a lanky cowboy, was methodically running up points.

"Don Siegel?" I said.

He failed to return a moderately difficult serve and shook his head in disgust.

He paused to tell me that this was a set for the Pat O'Brien movie about Knute Rockne. He also asked me if the shooting had been a joke. While he was talking, he managed to return an easy serve but lost the point.

"Can we talk?" I asked.

"Gee," he answered sincerely, "I'd like to, but I only have a ten minute break, and I'm playing Jim for a buck a point. I'd like to get some of my money back before we go back to work."

Jim was clearly one of the slowest ping pong players in North America, and I was in a hurry. I had also won a table tennis trophy when I was a kid in Glendale.

"Look," I said, "I'll give you a couple of quick games for a buck a point, and then we talk for five minutes. O.K?"

He pursed his lips and reluctantly raised his eyebrows in agreement. Jim handed me the paddle. We played quietly.

There I was with a head full of stitches, my gun missing, trying to keep out of jail and protect Errol Flynn from a killer, and I was playing ping pong. Siegel managed to stay in the game with some lucky shots and actually beat me 21 to 19. But I had the feel of the paddle back.

"Let's play the last game for two bucks a point," I suggested.

"Whatever you say," said Siegel.

The game lasted a little over two minutes. He beat me 21 to 1. He only gave me the single point to keep the game from being an 11 to 0 shutout. After that one point, the ball didn't slow down enough for me to see it or hit it.

Jim the cowboy grinned, and Siegel looked at me sheepishly.

I reached for my wallet to dig out forty bucks, but Siegel held up his hand.

"No," he said coming around the table and shaking my hand. "I was just keeping in practice. I haven't pulled a good table tennis hustle since I came to California five years ago. Let's talk."

Jim waved goodby. Siegel and I wandered over to the wooden bleachers and sat down.

"First, tell me where you were at two this morning."

"A party," he said with an amused grin. "Plenty of witnesses. You want some names?"

"No," I said. Since Siegel had been in sight when Flynn was shot at, he wasn't really a suspect.

"You were at lunch the other day when Flynn got a package."

Siegel looked at me expressionlessly.

"I'm working for Flynn," I explained, "investigating the attempted blackmail. You got a good look at the picture?"

"I saw the picture," he said.

"What did you think about it?"

"Well," said Siegel slowly, "I work a lot with stills. If someone had asked me, which they did not, I would have said it was probably a phoney. I'd like to see the negative, but even without it there were give-aways. Flynn and the girl were both looking toward the camera. It was too posed. And the man's body was wrong, out of proportion. I'd say the body was three or four inches shorter than Errol's."

I looked at the young man with new respect.

"Did you recognize the girl in the picture?"

He said he didn't, and I asked him if he remembered how the others had reacted.

"Peter, that's Peter Lorre, seemed interested, but nothing special. Flynn was amused and Adelman was upset."

"Beaumont?" I asked.

Siegel looked at me for a long time, pursed his lips thoughtfully, and then spoke carefully.

"He's a decent actor, a little showy, but pretty good. He did a reasonable job of hiding it, but he was shaken by the picture, badly shaken. Part of my business is watching actors."

"You'd make a hell of a detective," I said pulling out my notebook.

"If Jack Warner doesn't give me a picture to direct in a few years, maybe I'll look you up. How's the pay?"

"Rotten."

"Well, you can't have everything. I really do have to get back now. I've got a tough sequence with Walter Huston and I only get him for an hour. Stay out of table tennis games with strangers."

I went to Adelman's office. He had gone home to Westwood to get some sleep, but Esther put aside her reading long enough to dig out some information: Harry Beaumont had a Beverly Hills address on Dayton Way and a Crestview telephone number. I wrote them both on the back of an old business card given to me by a taxidermist who had needed my face to frighten a neighbor with a bad temper.

Beverly Hills was a wealthy suburb long before 1940. I felt out of place as I eased my Buick past well-tanned men and women in white on their way to tennis matches or golf courses. The cars were gigantic, new, or both. Everything looked bright and prosperous but me.

My information on Beaumont was minimal. I remembered him in a few roles, a tall, somewhat softly good-looking guy with dark, wavy hair. He'd start a picture tough and end up in reel five a mass of jelly, begging George Raft or Jimmy Cagney not to hit him. He certainly wasn't a star. I wondered where he earned enough to live in Beverly Hills.

Beaumont's house didn't give me an answer. It was big and white and stood alone on a hill with plenty of land and an ornamental steel gate and fence. The gate was open. I parked and walked up the driveway. Then I froze. Two massive Doberman Pincers had dashed at me from around the house. They sniffed at me growling, showing teeth and generally suspicious. I tried to say gentle things, but they weren't buying any.

After a full minute of this, a woman's voice called from the house:

"Jamie, Ralph, come."

The dogs backed off reluctantly eyeing my juicy arms and disappeared around the house. I walked slowly up the drive and to the door.

A woman in a light blue dress stood there with her arms folded. As soon as I looked at her, I had the answers to several questions.

The beautiful blonde woman in front of me was Brenda Stallings, a wealthy society deb of a little more than a dozen years earlier. She had doubled for Harlow and then had a short, successful film career before marrying an actor. The actor, I now remembered, was Harry Beaumont. Her money accounted for the home.

I had not seen all of her pictures, but I had seen her in the one in Charlie Cunningham's apartment that morning. The photograph of her and the dead blackmailer was in my pocket, and I touched it for luck. I also smiled.

"Yes," she said coldly.

"My name's Peters. I'm working for some people at Warners on a rather delicate matter. I'd like to talk to Mr. Beaumont."

"He's not in," she said starting to close the door. I stopped the door from closing with my hand.

"Then I'd like to talk to you."

"Remove your hand or I'll call the dogs."

With my free hand, I pulled the photograph of her and Cunningham and held it up so she could see it. She looked at it soberly and let go of the door.

"Please come in, Mr. Peters," she said. I did.

4

BRENDA STALLINGS BEAUMONT walked ahead of me without looking back, which suited me fine. I enjoyed watching her. Her legs were great and her yellow hair bounced softly on her neck.

Every inch of the floor was carpeted, thick white carpeting. We moved from room to room. The house was big, and each room was streamline decorated in brown, black or white or combinations. It looked like an R.K.O. set.

Everything was soft, plush and looked unlived in or on.

We stopped in a room the size of a tennis court. It was a kind of living room with two extra-long white sofas, three soft white chairs and a couple of black tables. A gold Oscar stood on one of the tables.

On the wall above a white brick fireplace were two huge painted portraits. One was of Brenda Stallings, bronzed and queenly in white. The other portrait was Harry Beaumont wearing a white jacket and a red scarf around his neck. He was looking down at me with his trademark, a combination of smile and sneer.

Brenda Stallings dropped lazily into an armchair and motioned toward one of the sofas in front of her. I sat.

"Well," she said looking at me, "I assume you are not soliciting for campaign funds for Wendell Willkie."

I had sunk uncomfortably deep into the sofa. I felt out of place.

"You said something like that in *Three Men,*" I smiled, "to Ronald Reagan."

"Something like that," she said without a smile, "but it was to Franchot Tone. You have the wrong studio. Now, what do you want?"

"Blackmail," I said.

Without looking at me she plucked a cigarette from a silver box on the table in front of her and put it to her lips. Then she reached for the Oscar which stood on the table in front of her. She raised it, touched something on the back and a flame spurted out of Oscar's gold head. She lit her cigarette.

"I didn't know you or your husband ever won an Academy Award? Is that a fake or did I miss something?"

She looked at the statue and not at me and blew a cloud of gray smoke.

"It's real, belonged to an actor who pawned it two years ago. We bought it and had it converted to a lighter to remind us how quickly fame and respect can be lost."

"Blackmail," I repeated, trying to shift to a comfortable position. There was none.

"I heard you," she said. "I have no intention of paying you for that photograph." She looked at me. Her eyes were cold blue, and very beautiful.

"You don't care if your husband sees it?" I said.

"Not in the least. Harry and I are separated and have been for some time. If you read the columns you would also know that we are past the verge of divorce. I don't think Harry would have the slightest interest in the photograph. I am willing to give you, say, $100 nuisance payment, but not a cent more, and if you don't want it . . ." She shrugged and pouted slightly.

I grinned. "You pouted like that in *Tortuga Bay* when Lionel Barrymore wanted you to sign away your father's ship."

"A fan," she said dryly.

"Why haven't you asked me where I got the picture?" I continued.

"You got it or stole it from Charlie," she said. "I rather expected something like this from him. Did he put you up to it?"

"I took it from his apartment," I went on.

"He won't like that Mr. . . . ."

"Peters, Toby Peters. I told you at the door. Charles Cunningham is dead, murdered, a 38 slug in his eye."

I watched her face. She took another gentle drag at her cigarette and looked at me without emotion. She shrugged again.

"I knew him for a few months. At first he was interesting. I liked his looks, his ambition and his confidence."

"And you got him a job at Warners with Sid Adelman?"

"Yes," she sighed. "Charlie Cunningham's death is of little interest to me. In fact, I am. . . ." She stopped and rose with her arms folded.

"You are what? Happy? Relieved?" I tried to stand gracefully, but sank awkwardly back into the sofa.

"I am going to ask you to leave. You can take the photograph or the $100."

"You misunderstood me." It was my turn to sigh and shrug. "I didn't come here to blackmail you. I work for Sid Adelman, and I am here to talk about blackmail, but not yours."

She sat again, cocked her head at me with curiosity and began to play with the Oscar lighter.

"Your husband was at lunch a few days ago with certain people at Warners when one of them received a blackmail threat from Cunningham complete with a photograph, not the one of you and Cunningham. Didn't your husband tell you about this?"

"We are separated, Mr. Peters, remember. Harry has not lived here for six weeks, and I doubt if he ever will again."

"Well," I said, finally pulling myself out of the seat, "I guess I'd better go find Mr. Beaumont. I may have to talk to you again. It strikes me as quite a coincidence that Cunningham was trying blackmail, that you knew him well, and that your husband happened to be at the table when the blackmail note came. Did you know Cunningham went in for blackmail?"

"No," she said, putting out her cigarette, "but I knew that he was ambitious and a miserable character in addition to being a liar."

"And a photographer," I added. She looked at me puzzled.

"Do you mind telling me your husband's financial situation?"

"Harry's career is doing very badly. The studio will not be renewing his contract. He has no money of his own and as soon as the divorce is completed, he will have no money of mine. His father has a slightly better than menial job, and Harry owes a great deal to a very impatient gambler in Las Vegas."

"Maybe not a good candidate for murderer, but how about blackmail?"

"No," she said, "He has no spine. He's perfectly typecast in his movies, but this really doesn't concern me, Mr. Peters." She looked at her wrist-watch and said, "Now, I'm afraid you'll just have to excuse me, I'm expecting someone."

"One last thing," I said, fishing into my pocket and pulling out the torn photo with the head of the girl. "Cunningham was pushing his blackmail with a photograph of a certain actor and a young girl in an indelicate situation. I have a photograph of the girl. Can you tell me if you ever saw her with Cunningham."

I handed the photograph fragment to her. She looked at it blankly for a few seconds and then handed it back to me.

"No," she said, tossing her golden hair, "I don't know that girl. Now, you'll have to . . ."

Something had changed, but I didn't know what. I did know she was suddenly very anxious to get rid of me, and I decided to slow things down a little.

"I'm afraid I have to ask just a few more questions," I said, taking a step toward her and trying to look determined. "It's either that or answer questions from the police. Cunningham has been murdered. You knew Cunningham. Your husband knew that blackmail was going on."

She glanced at her watch again and suddenly shivered and looked at me in a different way. I didn't know what was happening, but there was a change in her attitude. She had made up her mind about something.

"Mr. Peters; Toby," she said softly, looking intently at me so long that I wished I had shaved before I came, "there is something I want to show you, something important in the pool house."

She smiled and opened the door into the garden. I walked behind her, and she waited this time till I caught up. She leaned very close to my ear breathing softly.

"It is very important."

"I'm with you," I said, and I was.

The heart-shaped pool was as blue as her eyes, with a few wooden lounge chairs around it. We walked around the pool into the pool house, and she closed the door behind us. The light from outside flickered through a window bounced from the surface of the pool. The room was small, with a large white wicker chair and a black leather lounge. The floor was covered with dark carpet. There was a bar in the corner and the photographs on the wall were all of Brenda Stallings. They were stills from her movies.

On the lounge was the morning newspaper. GERMANY CONSIDERS INVASION OF ENGLAND, was the headline, and the story under it, with a photograph, was TROTSKY ATTACKED, DIES OF WOUNDS. She swept the newspaper and current history on the floor and motioned for me to sit on the leather lounge. I did.

She stood in front of me for about a minute and then, slowly and deliberately, unzipped her skirt and let it fall to the floor. Beneath it she wore a pink slip.

"Are we going swimming?" I asked.

She shook her head no and unbuttoned her white blouse. The bra matched the slip and her skin was tan and smooth. It was happening, but I couldn't figure out why and didn't want to ask. Brenda Stallings, the beautiful blonde who had appeared in front of me in theaters ten times her own size in love scenes with Gable and Freddie March, was looking at me as if I were Flynn.

"I don't get it," I said reluctantly as she bent over to unbutton my shirt. "I'm not giving you the photograph."

She smiled and finished unbuttoning my shirt. Then she leaned over and put her mouth against mine. She caught mine open. To say I was excited would be as useless as saying FDR wanted a third term.

"I don't want the photograph," she whispered.

She unzipped my pants and helped me out of them and then stood back to drop her bra and slip so that I could see her. Her breasts stood up and the hair between her legs was golden yellow. If she'd asked then, I would have gladly given her the photograph and the hell with the case, Adelman and Flynn.

I dropped my drawers and sat naked on the lounge looking at her as she walked toward me, the light from the pool reflecting against her browned body.

She leaned over me again gently touching the stitches in my head. Then she kissed them and pushed me on my back on the lounge.

"How did you break your nose?" she whispered, returning to my face.

"Accidents," I said, thinking of other things.

"You've had a violent life haven't you?" she said, her wide blue eyes inches from mine and her body on me.

"More than most," I said. I knew I was sweating.

She was up on top of me with a push, and I felt myself entering her. She was soft, wet and warm and moving rapidly. I was confused and barely in control. I don't know how I knew she was ready, but I knew, and it was just in time. I let go and she groaned happily. She leaned forward and kissed me again for a long time before getting off of me and moving away.

"That was nice," she said, putting her clothes back on.

I followed her lead and began to dress. I think I was shaking, but I don't think I showed it.

When I was dressed and standing, she moved close to me and put her arms around my waist. I put my battered nose into her hair and smelled perfume or sweat.

"We'll have to do this again," she said taking my hand and leading me to a door at the back of the pool house.

"The sooner, the better," I said. She kissed my cheek and opened the door. About ten yards in front of us was a gate. It looked like the rear of the house.

"You can go through there and around to the front for your car. Next time we'll meet at your place."

"I don't think you'll like it," I said, grinning at her stupidly.

"I'll like it," she said moving away and back to the pool house.

Then I heard the voice, a girl's voice from the house or the pool. I couldn't make out the words.

Brenda looked suddenly nervous and waved goodby. Something was strange. I took a step toward her and not toward the gate. She started to close the pool house door. I put my hand on it, and we repeated the scene we had gone through at the front door.

"I want you to leave, Mr. Peters," she whispered urgently.

"I thought I was Toby, and we were in love," I whispered back, forcing my way into the pool house past her. She followed me to the door.

On the other side of the pool, across from us stood a girl in a blue dress. She was looking into the sun and squinting at us.

She took a step or two toward us around the pool, and I could see that she looked about 14, a little older than she did in the photograph with Flynn. I fingered the picture of the girl's head I had in my pocket as she walked toward us, a slight touch of curiosity on her face.

"Mother," she said, looking at Brenda, "you weren't in the house, so . . ."

"That's all right, Lynn," said Brenda brightly. "Mr. Peters is from Warners. He was talking to me about a picture. Well, Mr. Peters, perhaps you could call me later, and we'll finish our talk. I think we can work something out."

She shook my hand and smiled as if nothing had happened. I had been taken, but not far enough. She had wanted me out of that house when the girl came home, and she knew the way to get me out. She hadn't batted an eyelash when I had showed her her daughter's picture.

"Your mother is a very fine actress," I said to the girl.

The girl looked childish and innocent. Her eyes scanned me, my clothes and my scars with some question about my credentials as a studio executive, but she was too polite to say anything.

"Brenda," I said, taking both of the woman's hands. "I've enjoyed our talk, and I look forward to hearing what you have to say later. I'll call."

"Please do," she said, guiding me back through the house. The girl trailed behind us.

As I stepped out the front door and down the stairs I looked back at the mother and daughter. The girl was shorter than her mother, and dark like her father. They both smiled and waved.

"I hope to see you again, Mr. Peters," Lynn said politely.

"You will," I said, with a wink and a return wave. Brenda was still smiling politely. The world continued to smile at me, and I didn't know what the hell it was all about.

As I walked toward the street, I heard the distant growl of the two friendly dogs. I hurried along and went out of the metal gate, closing it behind me just as Jamie and Ralph appeared. I didn't know if Brenda Stallings would have called them off this time, and I didn't want to find out. I'd had enough excitement for one afternoon.

5

MY OFFICE WAS IN THE FARRADAY BUILDING on Hoover near Ninth, not far from my apartment. I don't know who Farraday was, but the building bearing his name deserved to be condemned in 1930 or restored as an historical relic.

The Farraday Building was a four-story refuge for second-rate dentists, alcoholic doctors and insolvent baby photographers. My rent was paid not to the management but to Sheldon Minck, one of the dentists. I sublet a side office from Sheldon, who had been one of my first clients when I became a private investigator. I tracked down deadbeats who didn't pay their bills. I threatened to forceably remove their bridgework if they didn't spit up what they owed. I did pretty well until one fat woman in North Hollywood hit me in the face with a bottle of Fleischman's Gin. Sheldon fixed my teeth, and we had become something like friends.

There was an echo and smell of Lysol when I walked through the lobby toward the fake marble stairs. I could hear the faint snoring of a bum somewhere in the darkness. I ignored it and started walking up the three flights.

Very few potential clients came to my office. If a client called, I met him at his home or business or a cafe or coffee joint.

Fading black, block letters greeted me on the pebble glass door:

SHELDON MINCK, D.D.S., S.D.
Dentist

TOBY PETERS
Private Investigator

The S.D. after Sheldon's name didn't mean anything. He thought it might give him an edge with off-the-street patients. It was probably the only office in California where you could get your teeth filled and your runaway grandmother found in one visit.

I stepped into the reception room, which had just enough space for three wooden chairs, a small table with an overflowing ash tray and a heap of ancient copies of Collier's. I went into Sheldon's office where I heard the drill growling.

Sheldon was in his early 50's, short, fat, bald and myopic. His thick glasses were always slipping from his sweating nose. When he wasn't actively working on a patient, a wet cigar stuck out of his face. He had only one working coat which must have once been white.

Sheldon was working on a boy of about 10 who looked like Alfalfa in Our Gang. Sheldon squinted in my direction.

"Toby? Are you working or something? You've got calls all over the place."

He handed the frightened kid the drill, wiped his hands on his coat, shoved his cigar in his face and waddled over to a porcelain table covered with newspapers and x-rays of teeth. After shuffling through the pile, he came up with a torn edge of newspaper. There were some names and numbers on it:

Lt. Pevsner, call'd twice.

Adelman, three times.

"And," said Sheldon, rummaging through some drawers of teeth, "some wise ass called once and said he was Errol Flynn."

"What did you tell him?"

"I told him I was Artie Shaw, and I'd trade him two blondes for a redhead."

"Did he leave a number?"

"No," said Sheldon, fishing out a huge pliers. The kid in the chair gulped.

"Sheldon," I said, heading for my office, "that was Errol Flynn."

"No kidding?" He looked at me. "You know I once did an emergency filling for Cary Grant. He had great teeth. Paid cash on the spot."

"I'm glad to hear it."

Sheldon returned to the kid and took the drill from his trembling hand.

"And," he added, putting his cigar on the end of the small work table, "there are two guys waiting for you in your office. They got here about five minutes ago."

"Who are they?" I asked.

"Dunno," said Sheldon, pushing his glasses near his eyes and plunging the pliers into the kid's mouth. "I think I've seen them around."

I mixed a Bromo Seltzer in one of Sheldon's paper cups, listened to the kid moan for a few seconds and walked into my own office.

It is not much of an office. Designed as a dental room, it had a couple of chairs and my desk. The wall held a framed copy of my private investigator's certificate and a photograph of my father, my brother and me with our beagle dog Kaiser Wilhelm. I was ten when the photograph was taken, about the age of the kid who was screaming in the other room.

The two chairs in my office were occupied. I recognized both faces at once. One was the man who had saved Fay Wray from King Kong and the other looked like he could take on the giant ape.

They both stood up without smiling.

"You Peters?" said the burlier, curly haired and slightly shorter of the two, grimly.

"I'm Peters," I said pretending to go through the junk mail on my desk.

"My name's Guinn Williams, 'Big Boy' Williams. My friend is Bruce Cabot. You know us?"

"I've seen you," I said. After the pool house and Brenda Stallings, I wasn't about to be impressed by them.

"We understand that you know where a friend of ours is," said

Cabot. They approached me from either side of the desk, and I sat opening a letter from a Christmas card company. The letter said there was big money in Christmas card sales.

I looked up. Williams, who spent half of his screen time backing up heroes and the other half throwing fists at them, looked angry and ready to explode. Cabot seemed calm, but determined.

"Enough of this shit," hissed Williams through his teeth. He jutted out his square jaw and reached for me. Cabot watched. I had Williams' green tie in my mouth, and I could breathe his anger.

He lifted me up with one hand, and my face was inches from his.

"Son," he said, "you have thirty seconds to tell us where Princey is, or they're going to be cleaning you from the floor with toilet paper."

I considered kneeing him in the groin, but I wasn't sure it would bring him down, and I sure as hell didn't want to get him angrier.

"You'd better tell him," Cabot said evenly and reasonably.

"I don't know," I said. Williams was cutting off my wind, and the words came out in a gurgle.

"Wrong answer son," said Williams. Cabot shook his head sadly.

I had decided to put the knee to Williams and try to get to the door and Sheldon's office. Maybe I could find a forceps or a chisel for a weapon. Williams lifted me up and walked me to the window. I could hear Cabot calling a number on the phone.

"Bruce," said Williams, "He has ten seconds to answer or he goes flying down to Hoover Street."

"Let him say goodby first," said Cabot, handing me the phone. Williams reluctantly loosened his grip slightly, and I took the phone. The voice was familiar.

"Toby, old man," said Flynn, "how are my friends treating you?"

Cabot broke into a broad grin and Williams went from a chortle to laughter, tears coming to his eyes.

"This is some kind of gag?" I asked, regaining my wind.

"Something like that."

"Murder and blackmail and someone trying to kill you, and we're playing practical jokes?" I was angry and unamused.

"Ah, my friend," said Flynn, "that's the very time when amusement is most needed. My friends are there to help you if you need help. They'll do whatever needs to be done."

"O.K. maybe there is something they can do. Meanwhile, stay hidden for another day or so. I think I'm on to something."

"Fair enough," said Flynn lightly, and I thought I heard a female giggle on his end of the line.

"I thought you were going to go somewhere alone," I said.

"Well, old boy, I'd rather take the risk than do without. I subscribe to what Thomas DeQuincey, my favorite author, once wrote, 'I hanker too much after a state of happiness, both for myself and others: I cannot face misery, whether my own or not, with an eye of sufficient firmness: and am little capable of encountering present gain for the sake of any reversionary benefit.'" He hung up and so did I.

"Sorry about that," said Cabot.

Williams winked at me and grinned.

"You're a good sport," he said.

I thanked him and asked them to see if they could find out where Peter Lorre and Harry Beaumont were and then to take turns guarding Flynn, who seemed to have told everyone in Hollywood about his hiding place.

Cabot reached for the phone and made a call.

"Really scared you, huh?" said Williams proudly.

"Definitely," I said.

Cabot hung up and told me Lorre was at the studio and Beaumont was on location but would be back the next day. I thanked him, and Williams leaned over my desk to give me a friendly clip on the jaw. My jaw ached.

"See you buddy," he grinned.

"We'll keep an eye on the Prince," said Cabot, shaking my hand.

They left, and I looked at the names of the two people who had called me. Before I lifted the phone I tried to make sense out of what I knew. It didn't work. On my desk was Sheldon's Los Angeles Times. I read the important news. Cincinnati was still in first by 5½ games in the National, and Cleveland by 5½ in the American League. Big Stoop was bending iron bar to impress the Dragon Lady in Terry and the Pirates, and Lindy was making speeches urging us to stay out of the war in Europe.

I called my brother.

"Didn't you go home?" were his first words.

"You're my brother, not my mother," I said.

"Toby, don't start playing wise with me or I'll be over there with sirens. How's your head?"

"Fine. How is the family?"

"Let's not start that crap again. I want to see you in my office at eight tonight. You be here."

"I'll be there."

"The guy who got killed," said Phil. "His name was Charles Deitch. He has a record. Two years in Joliet in Illinois. Peddling pornography, statutory rape, attempted blackmail. You know any of this?"

"No," I said. I didn't know any of it.

"You're full of shit. Eight tonight. Be here."

He hung up and I called Adelman. Esther answered, but Adelman cut in on her.

"Peters, where the hell have you been?"

"Working on getting your negative and the money. I still have $200 coming from you."

"You remember what you told me this morning?" he said. He was not happy. "You told me that the fucking killer would destroy the photograph and negative and everything was fine? Well Philo Vance, you dumb sonofabitch, I got a call two hours ago. The price is up. Somebody wants $35,000 for the negative. You hear me?"

"I hear you. Was it a man or a woman?"

"A man, I think. He made his voice squeaky and high. He gave me one day to come up with the money. He's calling back in the morning. I don't care if he is a murderer. I've got to pay. We have full page ads in Variety this week for *Sea Hawk*. Newsweek ran a review with two pictures of Flynn. It's doing great in New York. We can't let anything happen."

"How about another murder?" I asked.

"What the hell are you talking about? You're fired."

"I'll work it on my own. The killer has my gun, and if I turn up that negative and your $5,000 you owe me $200. Besides, I've got a good lead. I know who the girl is in the picture."

Sid was silent. I could imagine his collar wilting as he looked up at the photo on his wall of the former junk dealers.

"You got a chance of coming up with something by tomorrow?" he asked.

"A good chance," I lied.

"You've got till tomorrow night," he said hanging up the phone.

I called Brenda Stallings. She couldn't see me tonight, but the next night would be fine, or the night after. I had a feeling I was being stalled, but I wasn't sure she had anything else she could tell me, and that is all I was interested in. She did offer me fifteen thousand dollars for the photograph of her daughter, but I told her what I had told Sid. It would be a bad buy. Someone had the negative and could grind out more prints faster than MGM could turn out Andy Hardy pictures.

I hung up and looked at my father, Phil, me and Kaiser Wilhelm. My nose was already flat in the picture, and the big kid with his arm around me might smash it even further later that night. My father looked down at us proudly. He had thought we would be brain surgeons or crooked lawyers or, at least, dentists. He had owned a small, not very profitable grocery store in Glendale till the day he died.

My brother had a family, a lot of debts and a mortgage on a two-bit house in North Hollywood. My father was dead. Kaiser Wilhelm was dead. Trotsky was dead, and I owned the suit I was wearing. I didn't even have a gun and I needed a shave. I decided to buy a gun, and a razor at Woolworth's.

My window went dark. I could hear the distant rumble of thunder over the hills. In a few seconds the rain started. In less than an hour my bad back would start burning around my kidneys. It always did when it rained. It had started two years ago. A giant black guy gave me a bear hug when I tried to keep him from getting to an actor I was guarding. Some muscles around my kidneys never bounced back.

I didn't feel very tough. I was tired and lonely and feeling damn sorry for myself.

Alfalfa was gone when I went through Sheldon's office.

"What was going on in there?" he said from his dental chair, where he sat reading the newspaper.

"Why didn't you come and take a look?" I said.

"I had a patient," he said, returning to his paper.

I went downstairs past the sound of the snoring drunk and ran to the cafe on the corner. It was dirty and I had to sit on one of those round red stools at the counter, but it was close and the rain was coming down hard. I had a burger, some fries and a Coke. Then I bought a safety razor and a toy gun at Woolworth's next door. I felt like an asshole and the girl who took my eighty cents looked at me as if she thought I was going to use the gun for a hold-up. She was about twenty, with a red mouth going over her lip line. Her dark hair was tight against her head.

"You remind me of Joan Crawford," I said seriously.

She smiled proudly, and I went to the door and dashed for my car. A green Dodge pulled out across the street splashing a man with an umbrella.

In twenty minutes or so, I'd be back in Burbank and, with a little luck, I'd find Peter Lorre. I hadn't put the pieces together, but I felt sure Harry Beaumont was important. Maybe Lorre could tell me something more about Beaumont's reactions to the photograph of his daughter and Flynn. I stopped thinking.

My back started to ache. I popped a Life Saver in my mouth, turned on the car radio and sang along with Eddie Howard, "I Found a Million Dollar Baby in a Five and Ten Cent Store." My windshield wipers were doing a lousy job. I turned off the radio, said, "Shit," and drove squinting through the rain. My back was in pain, and the green Dodge was fifty feet behind me. I was being followed.

6

THE RAIN KEPT COMING DOWN HARD. I drove with one hand while I shaved dry and managed to nick myself only two or three times. The Dodge stayed on my tail down Cahuenga, but it was far enough back and raining too hard to see who was in it.

It was after six when I pulled up to the Warner gate. Hatch came out with a red raincoat that made him look like a giant fire-plug. Rain was dripping from his hat.

"How's it going, Toby?"

"Fair, Hatch. You know Harry Beaumont?"

There was no car behind me, but I knew the green Dodge was waiting half a block down.

"Yes," said Hatch, "I know Harry."

"Seen him today?"

"No, he's on location, somewhere above Santa Barbara on a Walsh picture, *High Sierra*. Should be back tomorrow for some shooting, I think."

"Thanks," I shouted into the rain. "I don't want to be responsible for your death. Get out of the rain. Wait. You know where I can find Peter Lorre?"

"He's in something shooting over on Seven, I think." A bolt of lightning cracked toward Glendale and the Forest Lawn cemetery, a few miles behind the studio. Hatch hunched his shoulders and ran for the shelter of the shack, but he would be right out again. I could see a car pulling up as I moved in. I couldn't tell if it was my Dodge.

Stage Seven was easy to find. I knew the studio even in the rain, with four years between us. I checked myself in the rear-view mirror, decided I looked all right, patted the toy gun in my pocket, checked on the photographs and stepped into the downpour.

My back throbbed. I groaned slightly and moved as fast as I could.

The stage was silent when I entered. It was really a giant, barn-like building with sets built in odd places. Here a ship's deck, there a court room. I passed through a soda shop heading toward the rumble of mens' voices.

Working my way over sharp-edged electrical equipment, I found myself in front of a door. It wasn't radically different from the one that led to my office and Sheldon's, but this one said "Spade and Archer" in black letters on the glass. I walked around the door and the wall, past a reception area and into an office set. Standing near the desk deep in conversation were two men, both very short, both very animated.

They paused when I stepped into the room. Both were wearing dapper dark suits. The slightly taller of the two men advanced on me with a smile, a broad, familiar smile.

"I'm Edward G. Robinson," he said in a gentle, cultured voice radically different from the dozens of gangsters and cops I had seen him play. "This is Peter Lorre."

Lorre got down from the desk, gave me a slight smile and nodded while taking my hand.

"You're here about the picture," said Robinson guiding me to a leather sofa in the office.

"That's right," I said.

"I hope it wasn't too difficult for you to find us," said Robinson, "but we're both working late, and it is much more convenient."

"Sure," I said unbuttoning my jacket and wincing as I sat, from a sudden twinge from my back.

Robinson looked at me suspiciously from worn black shoes to wrinkled shirt and nicked face.

"We are interested in both pictures," said Lorre, with a slight German accent, lighting a cigarette and leaning against the desk.

"Well," said Robinson with a chuckle, "interested, yes, but committed, no. We'd like to discuss it first."

I wasn't sure how they knew about the pictures in my pocket or what their role was in all this, but I was going to hold out for as much information as I could get.

"Let's not haggle," said Robinson. "Mr. Lorre is prepared to pay $20,000 for both pictures. If that is not acceptable, he'll pay $11,000 for either one. That's my advice to him, and I think he'll stick to it."

"I'll stick to that," said Lorre in a low voice.

"What if they're not for sale?" I said.

Robinson and Lorre looked at each other.

"Then why would you come here?" asked Robinson, his hands stretched out.

"You are being very difficult, Mr. . . ." said Robinson.

"Peters, Toby Peters."

"Yes, Mr. Peters. The truth is we really want the picture of the girl providing we can examine it and be sure it's genuine. Mr. Lorre will pay . . ."

"Twelve thousand," finished Lorre.

"Come now, Mr. Peters," Robinson said with a friendly smile, sitting next to me, "you're dealing with two seasoned actors. We know how to wait."

"I'll let you look at the picture," I said reaching into my pocket, and you tell me if it's genuine."

"Fine," said Robinson with a grin. "We'll come out and look at it tomorrow morning."

"No," I said. "I've got it right here, but I'd advise you not to try to take it. I have a gun." I patted the Woolworth special in my pocket and pulled out the small, torn picture of Lynn Beaumont's face.

Lorre moved away from the desk and walked toward us. Robinson and Lorre exchanged confused glances. Lorre held out his hand, and I shook my head, no. I held up the photograph for him to see.

"What's this all about?" Robinson said somewhat angrily, standing.

"That's the picture you want to buy," I said, rising, with one hand on my toy pistol.

"Mr. Peters, if that's your name," said Robinson evenly, "if this is a Raoul Walsh gag, I don't find it funny. The picture we are dealing for is a painting, a painting of a girl by Modigliani and, possibly, another painting by Cézanne. Are you or are you not from the Frizzelli Gallery in Beverly Hills?"

"No," I sighed, "I'm from the Toby Peters detective agency, a one-man operation, me, and I'm investigating an attempted blackmail."

"Strange," said Robinson with a slight nod.

"I recognize the photograph," said Lorre. "I think I know what Mr. Peters is here about."

"Then, Peter, I leave it to you. I'm going to call and see what happened to the man from the gallery. I'll meet you later to deal with him." Then Robinson turned to me to take my hand, "My mistake, Mr. Peters. Please forgive me."

"My pleasure," I said, taking his hand.

He walked toward the darkness, away from the set and turned momentarily to speak to me.

"By the way, I think you should take care of that back. It could be something serious. If you'd like the name of a good orthopedic man, let me know. I used him myself when I took a bad fall in the death scene of *Bullets or Ballots*."

"Thanks, Mr. Robinson," I said, "I'll think about it."

"That means, no," said Robinson, disappearing into the darkness. "It's your back."

"Donald Siegel told me you might look me up," said Lorre, moving back to sit at the edge of the desk, "but until I saw the photograph of the girl, I didn't connect your name with the incident."

"Could I ask you a few questions," I said.

"Certainly," he answered, his wide eyes opening and his hand moving out expansively. "If I may ask you a few afterward."

"Agreed. First, do you recognize the girl in the picture?"

"No," said Lorre, "never seen her. Doesn't look like the type I usually see with Princey, but it's hard to tell."

"Can you tell me your feeling about how everyone reacted when the photograph showed up?"

"I was just finishing a rather mediocre goulash," he said, "when the envelope arrived. It was addressed to Errol. He took it, grinned and handed it to Sid Adelman. Sidney turned many colors, the most becoming of which was magenta."

I looked at him, but his face betrayed no hint of irony. I was sure he was enjoying himself.

"Well," he continued, "I took the picture from Sid, glanced at it, thought it was second-rate pornography—I've seen infinitely better in Germany—and handed it to Harry Beaumont, who turned in one of the worst performances of an undistinguished career."

"Siegel said he did a reasonably good job of hiding his reaction," I put in.

Loire shrugged. "I found it too broad. Harry doesn't think terribly well on his feet."

"You'd say Beaumont was upset by the picture?"

"Oh yes."

"Angry?"

"No, but upset, agitated. Donald took it next, seemed unimpressed and handed it back to Adelman. May I ask what has happened, or would it be none of my business?"

I told him most of what had happened, including the murder of Cunningham. I left out the session with Brenda Beaumont and the fact that the girl in the picture was Lynn Beaumont. I included the visit from Bruce Cabot and Guinn Williams.

Lorre sat quietly for a few moments.

"You know, Mr. Peters . . ." he began.

"Toby," I said.

"Toby, I have been in a great many murder films here and in Germany. I've studied the criminal mind somewhat, at least the devious criminal mind, since I have frequently been called upon to play deviates—have you ever seen *Crime and Punishment* or *M* or *Mad Love*?"

"Yes," I said. "*Mad Love*'s the one where you put on that stiff, mechanical costume and pretend you're the dead man. Scared hell out of me."

"Thank you," he grinned. "That madman would do anything for love. I would suggest, from what you have told me, that someone wants the photograph not for blackmail, but to protect the girl in the picture."

He had a point.

"But," I said, "someone, supposedly the murderer, made another blackmail call today."

"Ah," said Lorre, "perhaps you are dealing not with one, but with two people."

"Two people?" I said.

"The killer who wanted to protect the girl, and someone who got his wretched hands on the negative and is trying to continue Cunningham's blackmail."

"It's certainly possible," I said, "but in that case . . ."

"In that case," continued Lorre, advancing on me and taking my arm, "the killer will want desperately to get the negative and that picture in your pocket. And I would suggest that the killer is someone who loves that girl very much. Enough to kill Cunningham and make an attempt on Errol simply to avenge her honor."

We headed toward the darkness away from the dim night light of the set.

"Mind if I ask what this office is for?" I said, looking back.

"Not at all," said Lorre. "It's one of the first sets for a movie I'm doing. Should be shooting it in the near future. It's called *The Maltese Falcon*."

"I saw the picture," I said. "With Ricardo Cortez. Why make it again?"

"A very clever young writer named John Huston has convinced

the studio to do it with him directing. I don't know if it's a good idea or not, but it has an excellent role for me."

"This is something more like a detective's office that the one in the Cortez pictures," I said, "but it's still a palace compared to mine."

"That's what I wanted to ask you about," said Lorre, leading me to another set where he turned on an overhead light. It was a hotel room. "For background, can you tell me what it's like to be a real private investigator."

I sat on the sofa, and he sat next to me.

"By the way, this is a set for the movie," he said. "The detective, Spade, will sit where you are sitting. There's a very nice scene between him and—do you remember the Guttman character?"

"Yes," I said, "the fat man, but he wasn't fat in the Cortez movie."

"He will be in this one," said Lorre, "a very amiable gentleman from the theater named Greenstreet."

"Who's going to play Spade?"

"George Raft, I think," said Lorre, rubbing his eyes. "Please forgive me. I've been working rather hard, and I have to get back to another set. But can you tell me something about being a private detective?"

I rubbed my back and straightened up in the sofa. Lorre was looking at me intently, but I didn't have anything profound to say.

"It's a job for a lazy man with muscles and not too many brains," I said. "The pay stinks, most people think you're a few levels below a pimp, and the people you usually meet are welchers, petty thieves, angry runaway wives and husbands who try to belt you, alcoholics and other not-very-pleasant social types. The cops hate you; the clients don't trust you; and the people you look for or find would be happy to see you dead. I own an old car that's falling apart. My clothes are falling apart. I'm falling apart. I get hit a lot and I eat badly."

Lorre's eyes were wide.

"Fascinating," he sighed, "then why do you continue to do it?"

"Every once in a while, like now, it makes me feel really alive," I said. "It's something cops feel a lot, good cops, and private investigators feel once in a while."

I took his hand.

"Be careful, Mr. Peters," said the thin man holding on to my hand.

"I'll be careful."

The stage had been soundproof, and I didn't know if it was still raining. My watch said 7:30. I stepped outside, and it was still raining, but not as heavily. The sky was still a mass of darkness threatening to go wild again, and thunder rumbled far away.

I had half an hour to get to my brother's office. I decided to stop back to my apartment first. I should just about make it. I didn't want to carry a toy gun and the two photographs into a police station.

As I drove through Griffith Park my back continued to ache, and the green Dodge kept tailing me. There's wasn't much I could do about either problem.

At my apartment building, I parked in an illegal zone in front of the door and dashed into the lobby. The green Dodge pulled past looking for a parking space.

It would have been nice to take a hot bath, but I knew I didn't have the time. I didn't want to keep Phil waiting. He wouldn't understand. In addition, I didn't want to be in the apartment long enough for my friend in the green Dodge to find me. I had no gun. He may have had my 38. I had some pictures. He may have wanted them.

I turned the key in my lock, and the door flew open. I was pulled into darkness. The small light next to my bed went on, and I was thrown on my unmade bed. The sudden pull and the hard board under my mattress had done my back no good, and I had a feeling things weren't going to improve.

Three men stood over me around the bed. I'm giving them

the benefit of the doubt when I call them men. One was short, shorter than me, but built like a dark mailbox. He was bald and had no neck. He looked quite stupid in spite of his suit and tie. The second man I saw was grinning, but there was nothing funny. He was tall and slightly on the thin side. He wore a jacket, no tie and the meanest odor I'd ever met. The third man was familiar, but I couldn't place him. I wanted to remember their descriptions in case I survived. The third man was very big and broad, with grey hair and the smashed nose of a former fighter. It even beat my nose as a disaster area.

"No trouble, Peters," said the former fighter holding out his hand. "You give us the photograph of the girl and you stay alive."

His voice was deep and rasping, as if years of shouting had turned his vocal cords to gravel. It was very effective.

I managed to pull the Woolworth gun from my pocket.

"Sorry boys," I said trying to sound tough and confident, "but you are going to move across the room and sit very quietly while I call the police. And while we're waiting for them to pick you up on a breaking and entering, maybe you can tell me who asked you to pay me this visit."

They didn't move.

I aimed the gun at the mailbox, who neither moved back nor grinned. The tall grinner giggled.

Mailbox reached over and pulled the gun from my hand.

"The photograph, Peters, quick," said the croaker with the grey hair.

I sat up, started to go for my pocket and put everything I had behind a punch to the mouth of the mailbox. He took a step back, his mouth bleeding, while I made a move toward the door. My bad back slowed me up. The croaker grabbed me. I threw an elbow at his stomach. He turned and took it in the side, but held on. The tall grinner belted me in the lower back, over the kidney. He was either wearing brass knuckles or a roll of nickels in his fist. The pain in my back was electric. I moaned and slumped down. The mailbox moved toward me, wiping a touch of blood from the corner of his mouth with an ugly fist. I was going to be dead or very sick.

He pulled his tree-stump hand back to mash my face when the door burst open.

Bruce Cabot and Guinn Williams were standing in it. Cabot was grim, his arms out at his side. Williams was squinting at the mailbox.

The croaker dropped my arms, and I leveled a left to his groin. He went back against the wall.

Williams, his curls bobbing, went for the mailbox, who showed his teeth. Williams' closed fist thudded off the bald man's skull, and the stricken man went down, his head bouncing on my wooden floor. Williams shook his first and went for the down man.

Meanwhile, the tall giggler had stopped giggling and had pulled out a tall knife. He held it low as if he knew how to use it and had come up against other bellies before. He was behind Williams. Cabot reached out, grabbed the giggler's hand, pulled him around and grimaced as he threw a right into the man's stomach. On the way down, the tall man took a swing with the knife at Cabot, who backed away.

The grey-haired croaker was behind me pulling at my jacket and hitting me in the neck with his fist. I was trying to get back on my feet. Williams and Cabot pulled him off. The giggler and mailbox headed for the door.

"Let them go," I gasped.

The croaker was in good shape. He pulled away from the two actors and came up with a gun in his hand. It wasn't mine, but it wasn't a toy. The first shot missed my head, but I don't know by how much. It hit a lamp behind me. Cabot and Williams dropped to the floor, and Williams started up to go after the croaker who was leveling the gun at me again.

My hand touched something on the floor, the broken lamp.

The shade was demolished. Still on my knees I threw the lamp at the croaker. At ten feet, he wasn't likely to miss a second time.

The lamp caught him in the neck and head. The gun went off, the bullet smashing into my bathtub in the next room and making an eerie sound as it ricocheted.

The croaker fell backward with the smashed lamp and went out of the closed window. Glass flew across the room, and I felt a splinter hit my hand.

Williams and Cabot went to the window. It was three floors down and he might survive, but I doubted it.

"He's not moving," said Cabot.

"I didn't think he would be," I groaned.

Williams came back to help me up.

"What were you two doing here?" I said.

"How about, 'thanks,'" said Cabot, taking my arm and helping me to the nearest chair.

"Thanks," I said, "I think you saved my life. But . . ."

"Errol asked us to stay with you, keep an eye on you," said Cabot. "He thought you might run into trouble. He likes you."

"You driving a green Dodge?"

"Right," said Williams, "you spotted us?"

"Well, you're new at this. Now, you two better get out of here."

Cabot cocked his head:

"The police?"

"I'll tell them what happened, and they can come and talk to you if they want to," I said, looking at my hand. "If they call tell them you came to see me on business. Don't mention Flynn. Tell the truth about the fight." My hand was bleeding slightly. I took a handkerchief from my pocket. "The other two won't be back. They were hired muscle and brass, and the man who rented them is all over the sidewalk on Eleventh Street. Thanks, I mean it."

They left. I could hear noises in the street. The rain had stopped. A crowd was gathering around the body.

I reached for the phone and dialed my brother's office.

"Lieutenant Pevsner," came the familiar voice.

"Phil, it's Toby."

"Where the hell are you? I said eight. It's five after."

"I know. I'm going to be a little late."

"Oh no, you're not," he hissed.

"Then you better come over here and get me," I said, rubbing my kidney where the giggler had struck me. "I think I'm about to be arrested for throwing a guy out of my apartment window."

I hung up as Phil started to say, "Shit," but I let him get no farther than "Sh . . ." It sounded like a call for silence, and I needed a few minutes of that before I saw him.

7

BEFORE AN OVERCAUTIOUS BEAT COP made his way up to my apartment with a gun in his hand, I did a few things.

First, the photograph of Brenda Stallings Beaumont and Cunningham, or Deitch, if you want to be accurate, went into the pages of William Faulkner's *As I Lay Dying*. Remember, Bill Faulkner and I were in this together. Then, I put the picture of Lynn Beaumont's head in my wallet, back to back with a picture of my former wife. The toy gun went in a bottom drawer and a bandage went on my hand. Then the cop, a sweating, chunky redhead, found me calmly putting pieces of furniture in place.

At 9:30, I was sitting in my brother's office. The rain had moved south. If the giggler hadn't played hamburger with my back, it would have been back to near normal. My confidence was returning.

My brother made me wait half an hour. I wasn't about to be caught looking at anything on his desk, so I sat going over the whole screwy case. I didn't get anywhere.

At 10:15, my brother came in followed by a thin guy with a very white face, sandy hair and a gray suit. Phil slammed his door shut on the voices outside. It seemed to be a busy night for the L.A. police.

"This is Sergeant Seidman," said Phil, slapping his worn manila folder on the desk. "He's going to take notes on what we say."

Phil stood glaring at me.

"How's the family?" I said with a slight smile.

My brother's hand happened to be on a wire mesh box for memos. He threw the box in my direction. Memos, reports, photos and junk mail went flying. The box sailed past my nose crashing against the wall. The voices outside stopped for a few seconds and then went on.

Sergeant Seidman looked at neither of us. He pulled the second chair a few feet further from me and calmly sat down. Phil sat down too and pulled his tie even further open. He pointed a finger at me and turned pink.

"Toby, you just answer my questions. No jokes. No lies."

"Right," I said.

"Your full name?" continued my brother. Seidman lifted his pencil to write.

"Toby Peters."

"Not your alias," said Phil, opening the file. Then to Seidman, "His full name is Tobias Leo Pevsner. His alias . . ."

"My professional name," I interjected.

Seidman wrote nothing. He didn't give a shit for a family argument.

"You're a private investigator?" Phil went on.

"I'm a private investigator. Offices on Hoover."

I went for my wallet to get a business card. I still had a few thousand of them. They'd been given to me as payment by a job printer whose sister-in-law had stolen his 1932 Ford. I'd found her and the Ford in San Diego. It had taken me a week. She had done a bad job of disappearing with a delivery man. It's hard for people to suddenly disappear. You have to give up everything, every tie with your past, or a good cop or private investigator with a little time will get that string on you and pull you in.

"You want to tell us what happened in your apartment tonight?" said Phil with a smirk. He did not expect the truth the first time through. I wasn't going to disappoint him.

"I surprised three burglars going through my apartment. They overpowered me and threatened to kill me. They started to assault me when a couple of friends came by. Two of the assailants ran, and the other one pulled a gun. I threw a lamp at him after he took a couple of shots at me, and he went through the window. I can identify the other two."

"Three guys were burgling your apartment." Phil shook his

head. "Did they get lost in the rain? Maybe they thought they were in Beverly Hills or Westwood. What the hell have you got worth stealing?"

"Well, I do have a collection of matchbook covers and . . ."

"Who were the two friends who came to your rescue?"

"I'm not at liberty to say. They're sort of clients."

Phil clasped his hands together and looked at Seidman, who looked back at his pad and pretended to write something.

"You tell me who they were or you spend some lockup time," said Phil.

I smiled cautiously.

"You mean," I said, "you're not booking me for murder."

Phil ran his hand through his steely hair and touched his slightly stubbly chin before opening the manila folder in front of him.

"The character who took a dive out of your window was Martin Langer Delamater. You're lucky. He had a record going back to 1923. Twenty-two arrests and two convictions for everything from assault to attempted rape."

"Did he ever hold down a paying job?" I asked.

Phil cocked his head at me.

"A couple. Bartender, mechanic, security man . . ."

"Where?" I asked.

Phil grinned and spoke with mock amazement:

"Well, what a coincidence. He worked at Warner Brothers for two months in 1935. You were there then, weren't you, Toby?"

"Yes, I thought he looked familiar."

"And he came to your apartment by chance?"

"Maybe he was after my famous matchbox collection."

"Well," said Phil, sighing and removing his tie as he stood, "I think you and I are going to have to have a private talk."

"You get that down too?" I asked Seidman who, obviously, had not.

"Lieutenant," said Seidman. It was his first word and came out with remarkable confidence. "I'd like to suggest that you finish this interrogation as soon as possible. We still have the Maloney murder and . . ."

Phil sat down again and nodded in semi-resignation.

"Delamater was fired from Warner's," Phil said, "for theft. The studio didn't charge him, but before he went to San Quentin in '38, we ran an investigation on his past activities, and they were happy to tell us all about it. You want more coincidences?"

"Why not?"

"Cunningham worked for Warner's."

"Cunningham, who's Cunningham?" I said, looking blankly at my brother, who tried to look into my soul.

"The guy who got shot. The cute one with the bullet in his eye whose hand you were holding."

"I thought his name was Deitch?"

Phil actually smiled slightly.

"It is," he said. "He was using the name Cunningham, like you use Peters. And he had a job at Warner Brothers. Strange coincidence, huh?"

"Lots of people work or worked for Warner's," I said. "This is a movie town and that's a big studio."

"And," he jumped in, "a man with a rotten fake Italian accent answering your description was seen coming out of Deitch or Cunningham's apartment early this morning."

I shrugged.

"Lot of people probably fit my general description. Even you."

"Within twenty hours, you have been involved in two deaths, both of convicted felons, both of whom had worked for Warner Brothers. It's nice to get these people off the street, but we'd like to do it legally and handle it ourselves. Now you are going to tell me what you know about all this. You're not going to tell me stories about protecting labor leaders or surprising burglars. We'll start with your telling me who your two witnesses are. You're going to tell me in the next five minutes or you get locked up."

"On what charge?"

"Obstructing justice. Disturbing the peace. Suspicion of murder. Pissing in the park."

Seidman wrote quickly and passionlessly. My brother's fists were red, knotted balls with white knuckles.

"I'll have to ask my clients," I said.

Phil pointed to the phone on his desk, and I shook my head no.

"I'll call from a pay phone," I went on.

"There's one downstairs," Phil sighed. "Seidman will take you down."

"No. I go to an outside pay phone. Nobody listens when I call, Phil, or there's no deal. I've spent nights in the lockup before. I can do it again."

"Call me Lieutenant Pevsner. Steve, go with him and give him five minutes in the booth. No more."

Phil looked down at his folder and began reading, or pretending to. I picked up the wire mesh tray he had thrown at me and placed it gently on the desk.

Seidman opened the door and we went out.

The outer room was a lot more active than it had been earlier this morning. A woman with curlers in her hair was sitting at a desk with her arms folded looking at the ceiling. A cop was earnestly trying to tell her that there were no grounds for holding Frank, whoever Frank was.

Two uniformed cops flanked a thin guy wearing a sweater and a big, secret smile. He was either cuckoo, on drugs or simply drunk.

"Phil's your brother?" said Seidman, walking at my side toward the street. He nodded at the uniformed cop behind the desk in the lobby.

"Right," I said. "We love each other."

We went out the front door and Seidman pointed down the street. We walked. It was cool, and the sky was clear and filled with stars.

"You know about his older kid?" asked Seidman.

I said I didn't, and he told me that David, the 10-year-old was in the hospital, a car accident. The kid was going to be all right, but it had looked bad for week or so. There had been surgery, and the whole thing was sure to put Phil even deeper in debt than I knew he already was.

Seidman led me into a drug store and pointed toward a telephone booth in the back. He sat at the soda fountain where he could watch me and ordered a Green River.

I called the studio. Adelman wasn't there. I convinced the girl on the switchboard that I was working for him and needed his home number. Some woman with a young voice answered and reluctantly called Sid to the phone.

"You find him?" he asked immediately.

"Not yet. You hear from the blackmailer again?"

"No. You calling for the latest news? Turn your radio on and listen to Raymond Swing."

"Wait," I stopped him. "You ever hear of a man named Delamater? Used to work for the studio about five years ago, a security man."

"No, is he involved in this dreck?"

"He's dead. Tried to get the photograph of the girl from me."

"Schmuck," he screamed, "who told you to kill somebody?"

"I didn't kill him. He fell out of a window. Listen Sid, I haven't got time to talk. The police know Cunningham worked for Warner's. They'll probably be out to talk to you tomorrow. They've got me now, and I think I should tell them something or they'll lock me up."

"That would be bad?" he asked.

"That would be bad for you, because it would cut off the time I have to find the guy who's trying to blackmail you and bring you that much closer to paying off."

"Can you keep Flynn out?"

"I don't know," I said, "I'll try."

"You know he made the top ten box office list last year, top ten and *The Sea Hawk* . . ."

"You told me about *The Sea Hawk,* Sid, and Newsweek." Seidman was walking toward the phone booth. "I've got to go now. I'll get back to you tomorrow."

"Don't kill anybody else." He hung up.

"I'll try not to," I told the dead phone.

When we got back to Phil's office, I decided to do my best to cooperate. Seidman gave me an encouraging nod, but my best wasn't good enough.

"Who's your client?" Phil said, putting down his pencil and making a new effort at being calm.

"Somebody at Warner's," I said, "somebody fairly high up. He said I could tell you everything but his name."

"I don't give a shit what he said," stormed Phil, throwing his tie on the desk. "This is a case of murder, maybe two murders. I don't need your client's permission to carry on an investigation."

"But I do," I said. "Do you want what I have to give you or do you want to start throwing things at me?"

"Talk."

I talked. I said Cunningham had been trying to blackmail someone at Warner's with a photo. I had gone to make the exchange and been clobbered. The killer, I said, had gotten away with the photo and the money, and my gun. Phil wanted to know why the blackmail hadn't been reported to the police. I said that was my client's business, but I didn't think he trusted the police. Delamater and his two clowns had, I went on, probably come to my apartment to get me off the case. They were probably working for the blackmailer.

"You can identify the two who got away?" he interrupted.

"I told you I could, but I don't think they know who they were working for. Delamater looked like the thinker of the trio. He wasn't good at it but he was the best they had. Someone probably hired Delamater, who picked up the other two."

"Just the same," said Phil, "you go through the pictures and we'll try to turn them up. Now your story's fine. What I need are some names. Who is being blackmailed? Who knows about it? Who are the two guys who were in your place when Delamater went out the window?"

"The guys in my room had nothing to do with the case," I lied, "but you can check with them. They're Bruce Cabot and Guinn Williams."

"The movie actors?" asked Seidman.

Phil and I looked at him.

"Right," I said.

Phil made unveiled threats about my lying and had Seidman take me to the library in the basement. It was a musty room with two overhead 60-watt bulbs swinging from black cords. Seidman pulled out a pile of frayed, heavy green volumes, and I began to go through them looking for the mailbox and the giggler.

It took me over an hour. After a while the faces began to merge and look alike. Two or three faces looked exactly like mine, and dozens of them looked like Guinn Williams. But I found the two and indicated them to Seidman. The giggler was Judd "The Shiv" Chesler, and the mailbox was Steve Fagin.

When we got back to his office, my brother told me that Cabot and Williams had confirmed my story and would come in the next day to sign statements.

"Your client's name, Toby?" he said evenly.

"Two days, Phil. Give me two days, and I'll hand you the name and maybe the killer."

"You'll hand me the killer?" He actually laughed, but it didn't sound as if he were having fun. "You can't even hold down a job; you lost your client's money and your gun, and everybody beats the shit out of you."

"We all have bad days," I said.

"You're having a bad lifetime," he said. "Get out. You've got two days providing no one else gets killed."

I got up.

"Phil, I'm sorry about David."

My brother didn't look up. He just handed me my toy gun. "Don't shoot yourself, Sherlock," he grunted.

My car was in the same place it had been earlier in the morning. It had another ticket. I put it in the glove compartment and headed home.

There was a note on my door from the landlady. It said:

Mister Peters,
I am afraind I must ask you too move. You are paid entil the end of the month so you can stay till the end of the month and then you must leave please send me a check or cash money for damages to the apartment. Window, four dollars door two dollars for new lock lamp two dollars seventy five cents repair of wall from bullit three dollars repair of kitchen bathtub from bullit three dollars and thirty cents. Total of this is 15 dollars and a nickle.

Mrs. Eastwood

I took a hot bath, had a bowl of Shredded Wheat, checked to be sure the photograph was still in Bill Faulkner's book and went to bed.

In my dream, in color, I was walking down a Western street with six-guns on my hips. On my left, faithful sidekick Guinn "Big Boy" Williams gave me a wink. On my right, Bruce Cabot gave me a confident smile. We walked down the street and my big white hat kept slipping over my eyes. Advancing on us were six men, the giggler, the mailbox Barton MacLane, Henry Daniell, Claude Rains and Basil Rathbone. I didn't feel confident. I reached for my gun when the distance closed, and I realized that it was the Woolworth toy.

Rathbone shot me in the hand and I tried to tell everyone about my bad back. Rains took a second shot at me and missed. Just as I was about to go down in a volley of shots, Alan Hale leapt off a nearby roof. All six of the advancing men were crushed and Hale got up flashing teeth at me.

When I woke up, sun was splashing through the broken window, and someone was sitting in my only undamaged chair. The someone was looking at me. It was Lynn Beaumont.

8

THE GIRL LOOKED AROUND THE ROOM. I looked too. There was still some glass on the floor. The door was hanging loose. Two chairs were demolished. Pieces of ceramic lamp and a mashed shade were piled in a corner, and a small chunk was missing from the wall where a bullet had hit. Mrs. Eastwood's inventory had been correct.

Lynn Beaumont caught me looking at her.

"This place is a mess," she said with distaste. "Do you live like this?"

I sat up in bed, running a hand over my face and tasting the dryness in my mouth.

"Sorry, I would have told the Mexican maid to tidy up if I knew you were coming." I pulled my legs over the side of the bed.

"I called you during the day and last night," she said, glaring at me. "You didn't answer."

"I had a very busy night. Somebody tried to kill me."

She was unamused.

"Can you make coffee?" I asked, heading for the bathroom.

She couldn't. I tried toast. She thought she could handle that, but I remembered that I had no bread. There were no eggs either. There was some milk and a lot of cereal. I love cereal. I made the coffee while she glared at me.

I took a good look at her. She looked cute, clean and serious. Her dark hair was short and straight, and her dress was blue and conservative schoolgirl. She didn't fit the image of the girl in the picture with Flynn.

While I brushed my teeth and washed, I screamed some questions at her. She screamed back. She had tried to reach me at Warner Brothers. They had told her I didn't work there. Then she had tried my name in the phone book. I was there, the only Toby

Peters. She had called. I hadn't answered. So she got in a bus and came over from Beverly Hills. It wasn't a long ride.

"To what do I owe the pleasure of this visit, Lynn?"

"Please call me Miss Beaumont."

"Miss Beaumont."

Her glare was steady and stern. She looked determined and strong willed. Maybe that's what comes of having parents who are actors. The question was whether she had the strength of her mother behind it or something her father passed on to her.

"I don't want you to see my mother any more."

"Have to," I said, going for the coffee and pouring her a cup. "Part of some work I'm doing."

"What is your work?" she said sarcastically, accenting the word "work" with a slight sneer.

"I'm a private investigator."

The coffee was good and strong. She hated it. I poured us bowls of Shredded Wheat. She refused hers, and I ate both while we talked. I looked at the picture of Niagara Falls on the box. It looked cool, clean and far away.

"Mr. Peters, I know what you and my mother were doing in the pool house." Her hands were folded on the table. I poured out the last of the coffee. "My parents are getting a divorce, but I don't want . . . I mean, I don't think she . . ." She looked as if she were either going to hit me or cry.

"Miss Beaumont," I lied, "my interest in your mother is strictly professional. In fact, I'm on my way to see your father this morning about the case I'm on."

She didn't believe me.

"Have you made other visits like this to friends of your mother?" It was a long shot, but it couldn't hurt.

"Other visits?"

"You know a man named Charles Cunningham?" I watched her eyes. They filled with anger. "You know a man named Charles Cunningham."

"He is, was, a friend of my mother . . . like you."

"Was?" I said.

"They are not friends anymore. He promised . . ."

"What did you do to get him to promise?"

"Do? Nothing. I just talked to him and told him I'd tell my father and grandfather."

She seemed to be telling the truth, but she might also be a good actress.

"Was Cunningham friendly to you?"

"You mean did he try to get me in bed?"

"Something like that."

"I think he had something in mind, but I didn't let him get started." She looked firmly at me, but the tears weren't far.

"Have you ever done it with anyone?"

She shook her head no. I went on, finishing the coffee.

"How many times did you go to see Cunningham alone?"

She said she had gone to his place only once. He had made the one try and then had given up and tried to be friends.

"Did he give you anything to eat or drink?"

"Like coffee and Shredded Wheat?"

"Like whatever?"

The girl was beginning to think I was a lunatic. She looked around the mess of the room again and then at my face.

"He gave me a couple of Cokes while we talked."

"When was this?" I finished dressing; and she followed me, curious about the questions, as I looked at myself in the mirror. I still had a good chunk of the $200 left. Before I saw anybody else I had to buy a new suit, a shirt and a tie at a ready-to-wear place I knew on Hollywood. A former client owned the place. I had run a stake-out for him for five days. Someone was stealing his merchandise, one suit at a time. It was his brother. I got my $15 a day for the five days and two new shirts. I remembered it fondly as one of my better weeks in the business.

"Couple of weeks ago," the girl said.

"You got sleepy after you had the Cokes." It was my turn to glare at her.

"How did you know? I was sick. My stomach. It was a hot day."

"I'll bet it was," I answered.

"Huh?"

"Skip it," I said, "I spend most of my time talking to adults who keep trying to prove they're a little sharper than each other. It rubs off." She looked puzzled. "I was trying to be a wise guy," I explained.

To prove my good faith, I called Warner's while she sat there. Beaumont was not back from location on the Walsh film near Santa Barbara. The rain had hit all along the coast and ruined the shooting. They were going to stay one more day. I got the location and told Lynn Beaumont that I was on my way to see her father.

While she waited, I coaxed Bruce Cabot's phone number out of a secretary at the studio. Sid Adelman would have given it to me, but I would have had to take a lecture with it.

The girl continued to glare at me. While I gave the operator Cabot's number, I handed her a magazine. She put it down.

From Cabot, I got the name of the hotel where Flynn was staying, The Beverly Wilshire, and the name he was registered under, Rafael Sabatini. There were 800 hotels in Los Angeles. The one Flynn had picked was in the heart of the city on Wilshire Boulevard. It was not what I had had in mind as a hiding place.

Lynn Beaumont gave a maybe-I-was-wrong-about-you look, and I tried to look as innocent as my gnarled face would permit. I told her I had someone I wanted her to meet, and then I'd drive her home.

"Part of the case," I added.

"You have a gun?" she asked, still not sure I was what I claimed.

Looking as tough as I could, I reached into my jacket pocket and pulled out the Woolworth special. She was impressed. I slipped it back.

Fifteen minutes later, we were side by side while I knocked at the door to Rafael Flynn Sabatini's hotel room.

"Come in," he shouted cheerfully.

We walked in. He was being about as careful as a drunken mouse at a cat convention.

The room was big, but not a suite. The bed was massive, plenty of room for Flynn and the two women who were in it. They were both dark and looked like twins.

"Toby," Flynn smiled. He was wearing no shirt but fortunately, his lower torso was under the covers. "What have you found?"

"Errol Flynn in bed with two girls," I said sourly.

"Ah," he grinned. "DeQuincey . . ."

"How about saving DeQuincey for later, Errol?" I was business-like. The two girls simply looked at me and Lynn blandly. Lynn Beaumont's eyes were wide and her mouth open. Her sophistication had fallen.

"And," said Flynn looking at her, "who is this young lady?"

"You've never seen her before?"

He paused, still smiling, and touched his chin. Then he snapped his fingers. "The girl in the photograph, of course."

Lynn was totally confused.

"Toby," Flynn went on, "you are marvelous. Where did you find her?"

"Lynn," I said ignoring him, "have you ever seen this man before?"

"Certainly," the girl said.

"Where? When?"

"Where?" she stared at me as if I were insane. "That's Errol Flynn." She blushed. "I've seen all of his movies."

"Not all, my dear," said Flynn. "I was in an Australian version of *Mutiny on the Bounty,* and I did a thing in England I'd rather forget, back in '31, I think." His arms encircled the two girls.

"You've never met him in person before now?" I asked Lynn.

"No, never."

"Well," said Flynn, "I'm very happy to meet you now. Please forgive me for not rising to shake your hand."

I asked Lynn to wait in the hall for me. She looked confused, but obeyed.

When the door was closed, I asked Flynn if he had ever met Brenda Stallings Beaumont. He had, at a party, and had attempted to "strike up a friendship" as he put it. That was two years ago and she was not interested.

He knew Harry Beaumont, but not terribly well, and he didn't like him particularly.

"Actually, Toby," said Flynn seriously, "Beaumont is a bit jealous of me. We came to the studio at the same time, and I got the breaks. Between the two of us, I don't think he comes across on the screen with the kind of thing you need to get an audience with you. There's a softness about him even though he's big enough and can act. Do you think he had something to do with all this?"

"Maybe," I said.

"Am I to gather from the little episode we just went through with the girl that I am no longer in danger of being blackmailed?"

"Looks that way," I said. He flashed his teeth at the two girls who smiled back.

He jumped out of bed stark naked and started to put on his pants. I suggested that it might not be a good idea to go back on the streets, since the person who took a shot at him was still around.

"But, Toby," he said, advancing on me and putting a hand on my shoulder, "Mike Curtiz is having a Hungarian fit. I've delayed the picture and, I'm afraid, left the impression that I ran off to do something frivolous."

He nodded toward the two girls who stayed in the bed.

"Errol, I've got a good lead, and I'm sure I'll have this wrapped up by tomorrow night, the latest." I wasn't sure at all, but I didn't want Flynn out where he could get his head blown off with a bullet from my gun.

"You're right," he said, his lips moving into a firm line. "I'll just have to stay here another day or so." He started to take off his pants and said, "I've never starred in a mystery, but you inspire me. Someone just showed me a script, *Footsteps in the Fog.* I think I'd be some kind of a detective."

"One more thing, Errol," I said, my hand on the doorknob. "When Adelman finds out that the blackmailer has no weight, he will officially can me. I've had a run-in with the cops."

"Yes, Bruce told me," he said, climbing back in bed between the girls, "wish I had been there."

"Well," I continued, "I want to be able to say that I'm working for you if things get rough."

"Of course, old fellow," he said. "What's your fee?" He looked at the two girls.

I grinned.

"I'll take cash. $20 a day and expenses."

"You're working for Errol Flynn," he said with a wave.

I left without another word. Lynn stayed confused. I drove her home and left her at the gate. She said her mother was out. The dogs, Jamie and Ralph, escorted her to the steps where a Mexican maid was waiting at the door.

At this point, Charlie Chan or Nero Wolfe would have gathered everyone together in his office, trotted out the clues and exposed the murderer.

There was no room in this case large enough to hold all the people involved, the Beaumonts, Siegel, Lorre, Williams, Flynn, Cabot, Sid, the giggler and the mailbox. They'd be spilling over Sheldon Minck's x-ray machine. Besides, I didn't know who had done what to who and why. I was a first-rate, determined plodder with a hard head. That was the way I worked, and the way I liked it. Things were just too confused for a logical answer anyway.

Hy O'Brien, the owner of Clothes for Him on Hollywood, helped me pick out a conservative suit. No alterations necessary. I'm a straight 40 jacket, a 34 waist and 29 legs. I took a shirt and matching tie. Hy said I looked terrific and charged me half price, eighteen bucks. His brother, who was still working for him, gave me a friendly wave while he fitted a pear-shaped customer.

The ride to Santa Barbara wasn't bad. Actually, it was what the Chamber of Commerce calls scenic, but it isn't all that close to Los Angeles. I went beyond Santa Barbara to a place called Buellton, almost half way to San Francisco. The movie Beaumont was on was somewhere in the hills around here.

It was noon when I got to Buellton, and I ate a sandwich in a diner. The guy who served it wore a cowboy hat and a white beard.

"You one of them movie people?" he asked, serving me a hot mug of coffee.

"No, but I'm looking for them." The coffee was damn good.

"Back down the road," he said, pointing while he wiped his hands on a clean, white apron, "about two miles to your right. There's a road, says Miller's. Go up there into the hills. You'll find 'em. I brought them sandwiches yesterday. You think they appreciate a good sandwich?"

He never answered. I had a second cup, thanked him and gassed up at a Sinclair station. The Miller's sign was easy to find. I went up the road about four miles into the hills. A truck with some equipment passed me going the other way.

The location was against some high hills, nearly mountains. The director was shouting at someone dressed like a state trooper. The director wore a cowboy hat and an eyepatch.

Ida Lupino, carrying a dog, walked near me, and I asked for Harry Beaumont. She looked around and directed me toward a young man who said he had seen Beaumont, talking to an actor named Cowan. He pointed out Cowan, who was leaning against a tree, smoking. I recognized him. He was thin, taller than me, with a pencil-line mustache and hair thin and combed straight back.

"Jerome Cowan?" I said sticking out a hand.

"Right," he said, shaking my hand.

"I wonder if you can tell me where to find Harry Beaumont?"

Cowan looked at me quizzically.

"I'm a private investigator working for the studio on something rather confidential," I whispered.

"Really," he said, "I'm playing a private detective in my next picture."

We talked for a few minutes, and he said he was going to play Miles Archer, Sam Spade's partner in *The Maltese Falcon*. It wasn't a big role, but it was a good one. I told him about my meeting with Peter Lorre. It wasn't much of a coincidence since Warner character actors appeared in many pictures in a year. He didn't know where Beaumont was, but he knew someone who might.

"Beaumont just had a few unpleasant words with Bogie," said Cowan, "maybe he knows which way your man went."

I thanked Cowan who told me they were on a shooting break and Bogart was probably halfway up the hill. I started up the hill toward a knot of people, one of whom was talking rather loudly in a voice I recognized, a near-angry lisp.

"Try it again, one more time," growled Bogart.

I was close enough to see a wirey little guy in a state trooper's uniform lunge at Bogart, who laughed, jumped on top of the man and went tumbling with him into a tree.

"That's one out of two," said Bogie his back against a tree and panting. "Let's leave it at that."

The state trooper and two other men and a skinny woman carrying a script started down the hill. As I moved toward Bogart, he looked up at me.

"Don't tell me," he said lifting his upper lip in a familiar grimace of thought. "Peters, Toby Peters, used to work security at the studio." He started to get up but I motioned him back, took his hand and joined him against the tree. "Where you been?"

"Private investigator," I said. He nodded and lifted an eyebrow. Bogie had always looked either very gentle to me or very rough. There was no inbetween. Right now he looked rough as he nervously touched the lobe of his left ear. His hair was shaved at the sides and he seemed a bit jumpy.

"It's been a while," he chuckled. "Last time I saw you you were helping me into a car after a party where I was saying a few things to the brothers Warner that I would have regretted in the morning. You back at the studio?"

"No," I said looking up at the mountain. It looked rugged.

"Yeah," he said seeing my eyes move up. "It's a bastard all right. This Walsh is some character. I've spent five years making movies on Warner sets that looked like everything from a roadhouse to the yard at Alcatraz. Now, I get a nut who gets me to shave my head and climb mountains. I really think he'd like it if one of us fell as long as the camera was moving."

"Rough," I said sympathetically.

"Hell no," he laughed slapping me on my shoulder. "This is a big break for me. It's a good part, might even put me up with the big boys on the lot." He put his thumb up and gave me a wink and then pulled a silver flask from his pocket. He extended it to me with uplifted eyebrows of invitation. Then he stopped.

"I remember," he said. "You don't drink. A beer once in a while."

He drank himself and got to his feet. I joined him and realized that he was about my height and a little on the thin side. I'd seen him in some films since I left the studio and had started to think of him as tall and burly when I knew he was average and thin. As a cop, I had seen dozens of victims identify their robbers, rapists and loonies as a foot taller and fifty pounds heavier than they really were. I knew that for his height and weight Bogie could be rough, and I also knew from experience that he was willing to face uglies who met the descriptions of those robbers of my cop days.

Bogart stretched, put his hands on his hips and looked up the hill.

"It's a long one, but I think George made a mistake in turning it down," he said. I figured George was George Raft. Bogart confirmed it with his next words. "Now if old George will just turn down the Falcon role it'll be a good year's work for me."

From about 100 yards down the mountain, a man's voice echoed into the rocks.

"That's enough vacation, you lazy clown. It's time we got you killed. Get ready to die in 15 minutes."

"Walsh," shouted Bogie, "you one-eyed baboon. I'll die for you, but I'm not taking the tumble from up there."

"Fifteen minutes," shouted Walsh.

Bogart was shaking his head and smiling when he turned back to me.

"You know that maniac actually carries a gun on the set?" he said tilting his head toward the crowd of small people below us. "You're a private cop; you carry a gun?"

"Sometimes," I said, "but about half the time it's a dime pistol from Woolworth. I've got to get going, Bogie. Fella down the hill said you might know where I can find Harry Beaumont."

The name did something to the actor. His jaw tightened and his cheekbones quivered.

"The man's got problems," he said. "I can understand that. I've had a few myself, but he's carrying a big cow chip on his shoulder and I'm going to take it and smash it in his kisser."

Bogart's anger was on the surface and ready to explode. It had come fast and I stepped back. He saw what I had done and the fire, steam or dry ice in his eyes cooled suddenly.

"Come on," he said touching my arm. "I'll take you to him. What'd he do, murder a crippled newsboy?"

As we started down the hill I gave him just enough to answer his question and not enough to lead to details. He knew there was something I didn't want to say and he respected it.

We passed the director wearing an eye-patch and a cowboy hat.

"Where are you going Edwin Booth?" cackled Walsh.

"My friend and I are going to the latrine together," Bogart said in a high falsetto. Walsh and the group of actors and technicians around him broke out laughing.

"And my family wanted me to be a polo player," whispered

Bogart leading the way toward a farmhouse about fifty yards away. Bogie explained that the farmhouse was being used for costume changes. Beaumont had already finished his shooting for the location and was on his way back to L.A. by now if he had changed quickly.

The farmhouse was small. Bogart knocked and a voice told us to come in.

Harry Beaumont was facing us and looking none too happy about it. He was dressed in a state trooper's uniform.

"What do you want?" He was a big man, but I thought I could take him. A look at Bogart made it clear that he was quite willing to test the bigger man on the spot. Beaumont's fat was beginning to show and his skin was loose on his hands and face.

"Harry, this is a friend of mine, Toby Peters," said Bogart. "I'd appreciate it if you'd answer a few questions for him."

"You know what you can do with your appreciation," Beaumont snarled.

Bogart pointed a finger at the bigger man and spoke softly.

"And you know what you can do with a mouthful of loose teeth." He turned from Beaumont to me with an amused look and whispered. "Sorry, that's the best dialogue I could come up with on short notice. It lacked a certain flair wouldn't you say, Toby?"

I shrugged. I had a couple of good answers, but it was Bogart's scene and he was enjoying it, playing with Beaumont to keep tension from turning to flying chairs.

"Stupid bastard," Beaumont said under his breath.

I could see Bogart tense, and reached out to put a calming hand on him. My hand didn't calm him. What did stop him as he took a step toward Beaumont (who had turned his back) was a voice from outside the house calling Bogart for the next scene.

He pulled his eyes away from Beaumont's back and turned to me. He sighed, knowing that his moment to break a knuckle on Beaumont's skull was moving away from him.

"Toby, take care of yourself and my little pal Beaumont here."

Beaumont grunted, his back still turned. Bogart ruffled my hair, smiled and went out.

When the door closed, Beaumont turned and looked at me with his patented sneer.

"In a year," he hissed, "he'll be where I am, bit parts in B pictures."

"I'm fascinated by your predictions," I said, "and I'd like to hear more, but you and I have some business. I'm a private investigator working for Errol Flynn."

"I'm impressed," he said sarcastically.

Maybe he knew nothing, but he could be the key to this whole thing—the guy who took a shot at Flynn and murdered Cunningham over his daughter's honor. He didn't seem the type, but I'd been fooled before. Getting him angry was the quickest way to get information and Bogart had given me a good start on the job.

"You were at the table when Flynn got that blackmail threat?"

"You came all the way out here to confirm that?"

"No, I came all the way out here to ask you what you did when you recognized the girl in the picture."

He wasn't as good an actor as his wife. His look was narrow and wary.

"Recognized the girl?"

"Your daughter, Lynn."

He walked toward me. I was ready for him if he didn't have my gun in his pocket.

"You mind telling me what you've been doing for the past two days," I said evenly, "like every minute of your time, and what you know about the murder of a guy named Cunningham?"

He fingered his moustache.

"Not at all," he said. "I have nothing to hide."

He started to turn and I relaxed slightly. It was a mistake. I was making a lot of them. He turned quickly for such a big man and rammed his fist into my stomach. I doubled up, trying to refill my lungs. Beaumont pushed me backward with both hands, and I slid down catching a little air, but it was coming too slowly. He opened a closet and shoved me in. I reached up to hold the door open, but a coat was in my mouth. The door closed and I heard Beaumont's footsteps moving away. As I untangled myself from the clothes and got to my feet, I heard a car start and pull away. There wasn't much room in the closet to get my shoulder into the door. I sat in the dark with my back against the wall. It took two or three good kicks to break the lock, which wasn't designed for holding men.

As I ran out of the house, I met Cowan coming down the hill. Behind him and in the distance I could hear Bogart shouting, "All right. All right. I'll take the goddamned fall."

"You talk to Beaumont?" Cowan asked me.

"Briefly," I said panting.

"Mean-tempered son of a bitch, isn't he?"

Cowan told me Beaumont had torn down the road in his car, a white '39 Cadillac. I thanked him and made it to my car, which was no match for a Caddy. My wind was back, and I wanted my hands on Beaumont. I had been pushed around enough

9

BEAUMONT HAD A THREE or four minute start on me. He also had a Caddy that could leave my gasping Buick eating dust all the way back to Los Angeles.

But I had a few things going for me. First, that big car of his ate a lot of gas, and my tank was full. If he needed gas anywhere between Buellton and just beyond Santa Barbara and he stayed on the main road, I might catch up with him.

I knew I was a good driver. I didn't know anything about Beaumont except that he lost his temper easily. That might make him a driver who took chances. Maybe he would get caught in a speed trap or maybe he'd have an accident. He was still wearing his state trooper costume from the movie. He might stop to change that if he thought I hadn't followed.

I went down the mountain. Between some lower hills I saw the white Caddy heading down the highway. He was going way past 70. I took it easy going out of the hills, but pushed the speed limit all the way and never let up when I hit the highway.

He wasn't in sight for forty minutes, and I was beginning to think he had turned down a side road or held back waiting for me to pass. Then I spotted him. He was a couple of hundred yards ahead in a gas station, a ramshackle place with the ocean at its back and a mountain in its face, on the other side of the highway.

Once Beaumont was gassed up, he would almost certainly not stop again till he hit home. When he got to the city I either closed the gap or took a chance on his seeing me. He didn't know what my car looked like, but I was sure he'd remember my face.

I stepped on the gas and pulled into the station on the other side of the pumps from the white car. Beaumont wasn't in it, but an attendant was pumping it full of ethyl.

The attendant looked like an extra from a Republic Western, one of the tough bad guys. He was wearing Levi's, a red flannel shirt and a two-day growth of beard. His hair was long and black, and he was a burly type.

"What can I do for you?" he asked.

"Check the oil," I said, getting out of the car and stretching. I couldn't see Beaumont.

I tried the washroom inside the station. The door was open, but Beaumont wasn't in it. I considered asking the attendant where the driver was, when I saw the small house behind the station. It was a little more than a shack, but it was right on the edge of a two-story drop into the ocean. The view probably made up for the lack of splendor in the house.

Moving around the far side of the garage I came up on the shack. There was a dirty window. I went up to it as quietly as I could through the thick weeds.

Through the window I could see Beaumont in his state trooper uniform. He was talking on the phone. I put my ear near the window to try to catch what he was saying. The noise of the ocean drowned out his voice.

I went to the front door and opened it a crack.

". . . when I get there," he was saying. He paused and laughed. It was an ugly laugh, the laugh of a man who knew the person dealing with him hated him, but he was going to rub the hatred back in that person's face.

"I know what I am," he went on. "We've been over that before, several times. We also know what you are, don't we? But that's not what I want to discuss." Another pause for the person on the other end to talk. "I don't think that would be a good idea. The fewer people involved, the better. I . . ."

The interruption wasn't on the phone. It came from me. Something grabbed me from behind and shoved me into the room. I kept my balance, and Beaumont looked up.

"Caught him listening to you at the door, trooper," said the gas station attendant, who had given me the shove. He stood across from me with a heavy chisel in his hand.

Beaumont held the phone for a second, uncertain, his mouth open.

"I'll see you in a few hours," he said into the mouthpiece and hung up. Then to the burly gas station man, he rasped:

"Good work. I thought he looked suspicious down the road. I think he's on our wanted list."

"Hold it," I countered, moving toward Beaumont.

The gas station man held up the chisel. Both he and it looked mean.

"You hold it, mister," he said. "You want to take him, trooper?"

"No," said Beaumont with a triumphant, one-sided smile. "Hold him here for about fifteen minutes. I'll be back with a car and some help."

"He's not a state trooper," I shouted. "That's a costume for a movie. He's an actor."

Beaumont had recovered and was now playing the part. I had to admit he looked like a trooper, and I surely looked like a thug from a Monogram serial. Beaumont adjusted his cap, patted the bearded man on the shoulder and took a step toward the door.

"Why's he driving a new Cadillac if he's a state trooper?" I tried.

Beaumont laughed and shook his head sympathetically.

"Not very clever," he said, "that's a stolen vehicle. I'm driving it in. My partner is in my car about ten minutes ahead of me."

"That's good enough for me," the gas station man said.

Beaumont went out of the door.

"Why didn't he call from here?" I tried on the man with the chisel.

"He could see I could handle you."

"But he was on the phone when I came in. Who was he calling? Why . . ." I could hear the Caddy starting above the sound of the waves.

"Did he pay you for the gas?"

The man shook his head. His shoulders were broad. He looked as if he regularly lifted motors for sport.

"I gotta hand it to you fella," he said. "You don't give up. Now why don't you just sit down and wait for the trooper to come back like a good guy, huh?"

I looked around the room, but it didn't inspire me. The table, cabinets and bed all looked homemade and not very well or carefully made.

"What's your name?" I asked, sitting on the bed.

"Burt." Burt kept holding the chisel over his head. "I don't need to know yours."

"I'll tell you anyway. It's Peters. I'm a private investigator, and I was following that man. He's involved in a murder."

"Jesus," sighed Burt, "you don't give up, do you?"

"My identification is in my wallet, in my pocket." I reached for the wallet.

"Don't prove anything," Burt replied, as I pulled out the wallet. "Might all be fake."

"Burt, you are going to find out in about twenty minutes that I have been telling you the truth because no state troopers are coming back here. The trouble is that when you apologize it will be too late, and I'll have to try to find that man in Los Angeles, which is not easy."

"Talk all you want, mister, just don't move."

I sat forward. Two minutes or so had passed since Beaumont went to the door. I looked around the room at the furniture and a tire company calendar on the wall. I leaned forward with my head in my hands, but I wasn't relaxing. Burt was going to have a hell of a time standing over me at attention, but in a few more minutes it wouldn't matter. Beaumont would be so far gone that I might as well just wait it out.

A car pulled into the gas station outside. Burt heard it first. He was used to the ocean. He turned his head toward the door, unsure of what to do. I ran at him head down. His arm with the chisel was up.

My head hit him in the stomach, and the chisel went flying. Burt was gulping for air and holding his stomach with both hands when I straightened up. I considered hitting him to be sure he'd stay off my back, but I didn't have the time or the desire. Beaumont was simply a better liar than I was a teller of truth. His whole career had been built on convincing people that he was someone else. My career was based on convincing people that I was a responsible character named Toby Peters.

I ran through the weeds to the station and my car. The hood was up. I slammed it closed and jumped in. An old lady in a DeSoto tried to tell me she wanted two dollars worth of gas. I ignored her and took off.

Burt staggered out of the shack as I pulled away. The old lady tried to get him to listen to her order, but he was following me out into the road.

Beaumont had a good enough start on me to beat me back with no race now. But I still had a possible ace. He might feel confident enough of his performance to think that there was no hurry. He might even stay inside the speed limit. I pushed my Buick over the limit, put my foot to the floor and felt it rattle as I began passing law-abiding citizens.

Within ten minutes I saw the Caddy in front of me. We were alone on a stretch between rocks. Beaumont spotted me around a turn, and I figured him to try to outdistance me. Beaumont had something to hide, and from the way he was acting, it probably was something he had in the car with him. It might be too much cash or a gun of mine or a negative.

I was wondering about who he had called, back at the shack, when I lost sight of him for a second or two behind a turn. When I came through the turn and could see around the formation of rock, he was gone.

I braked and pulled over. A cloud of dust was settling a few dozen yards ahead. I could see a small road. I got back in my car and moved forward. I turned up the road slowly and heard an engine go mad in front of me.

Beaumont's Caddy was coming back down the narrow road toward me, and he was coming fast. We were going to hit head on, and the momentum, if not good sense, was on his side. I threw the Buick in reverse and started back. Before I turned to look at the road I could see Beaumont's face under the trooper's cap. He was not in a friendly mood.

I didn't know if anything was coming down the highway, but I didn't have time to worry about it. Going as fast as I could in reverse, I shot across the two-lane strip.

A small truck barely missed me, and I went backwards off the road and hit my brakes. Beaumont skidded behind the truck and looked back at me.

One of my wheels was spinning over the edge of a drop into the ocean. If Beaumont turned around and rammed me even gently, I'd go over. He might have had it in mind, but the truck that had barely missed me stopped about fifty yards ahead, and the driver got out.

I kept spinning my wheels. The truck driver had his hands on his hips and was yelling back at us. Beaumont decided to forget the ram and head toward L.A. and his secret meeting. The truck driver hurled some great quotes down the road and left.

The Buick wouldn't move forward. I gunned it, coaxed it, and cursed it, but it wouldn't move.

I got out and walked in the direction of Los Angeles. About a mile down I found a truck stop. I had a cup of coffee and waited for a guy in the garage to take a tow truck out and pull me off the ledge.

The guy in the tow truck talked all the time, but I didn't listen. My mind was on Harry Beaumont. I didn't even think of the case or the money. I just wanted to sink my fists into that man's face. When I was a kid, I used to break the wishbone with my brother on Thanksgiving and wish for a million bucks or a Tris Speaker baseball glove. I daydreamed that I had the long part of that bone, and I wished for Beaumont in front of me. The wish kept me going all the way back to Los Angeles.

10

FINDING BEAUMONT AMONG THE MILLION and a half people in Los Angeles was not as easy as I hoped it would be. I should have figured he would find a hole. Holes were easy to find in Los Angeles, the largest municipality in the world. The city was really 451 square miles of suburbs loosely strung together. The original Spanish name for this mass was appropriately ponderous: El Pueblo de Neustra Senora La Reina de Los Angeles de Porciuncula. The studio had only one address for Beaumont, the one in Beverly Hills. I called Brenda Beaumont. The Mexican maid said she wasn't home. She said Lynn Beaumont wasn't home either.

I had a burger at the Carpenter's Drive-In sandwich stand on Sunset. The waitress was a skinny woman with a fake smile.

Then, I headed for Dayton Way in Beverly Hills. My idea was simple; scare the shit out of Brenda Beaumont and get her to give me a lead on her husband.

It was still light when I pulled up in front of the gate of the Beaumont house. But I didn't stop. There was a white '39 Cadillac in the driveway. Harry Beaumont was home. I parked about fifty yards down in the shade of a short palm. Beaumont came out in about five minutes. He was wearing a white suit and an angry scowl.

Following him in traffic was easy. He was a lousy driver, easy to anticipate, and he had no idea he was being followed. We drove back to Hollywood, or what's called Hollywood. Hollywood isn't a separate place but a district in the city on the foothill slopes of the Santa Monica mountains. The movie studios aren't even located there, except for Columbia. When Beaumont pulled into a parking lot on Franklin off of Hollywood Boulevard, I turned into a small lot on the other side of the street. The old guy in the lot was wearing a blue uniform that didn't fit. He looked like an ancient kid playing policeman. I handed him my keys and a five-dollar bill and hurried back to the street. Beaumont came out a few seconds after I did and went into one of those buildings that couldn't make up its mind if it was a hotel or an apartment.

The place was called "Aloha Palms," but there were no palms. There was a kind of lobby with a desk. Beaumont bypassed the desk and the man behind it and went for the stairs.

My suit was new, my stomach was full, and I was anxious to meet Harry Beaumont in a nice quiet place for a talk. I walked into the lobby of the "Aloha Arms" slowly, looking around as if everything had a slight odor. The guy at the desk pretended not to see me. He went on listening to Baby Snooks on his radio. He was young and skinny, with plastered down hair and a bad complexion. He also looked a bit stupid. I flashed my tin, a private investigator's badge I bought for a quarter three years earlier.

"Pevsner," I said, "Homicide." I leaned forward over the desk. Fanny Brice had just finished playing bridge with Robespierre, her little brother. She had placed him between two chairs and walked over him. The clerk didn't smile. I didn't smile.

"Yes, sir," he said.

"Man who just walked in here," I whispered, "who is he, and what room is he in?"

"Mr. Simmons is in Apartment Fourteen." He touched a pimple.

"Did he kill somebody?"

"Sorry, I can't talk about it. Does he have many visitors?"

"I don't know about days," said the kid, "I'm nights. I haven't seen him with anyone during the nights. He's only been here a few weeks. Can I tell Mr. Siska about all this? He owns the Aloha Arms and . . ."

"Let's keep it between you and the Homicide Bureau for now," I said, reaching over to pat his shoulder and give him a wink. Siska might be a lot brighter than my acned friend, and I didn't want my description given to Homicide.

Baby Snooks screamed "Daddy," and I headed for the stairway.

Beaumont's room was at the end of a hall on the second floor. I wrapped my hand around my keys and made a fist. Then I knocked. No answer. I knocked again, louder. Nothing. The door was locked. There was another door at the end of the hall. Outside the door was a fire escape.

What looked like a window to Beaumont's apartment was about four feet from the fire escape. The window looked as if it were open a crack.

I couldn't quite reach the window, but it was only a short jump. I was less worried about the fall than the possibility that Beaumont might be inside, hear me and greet me as I pulled myself in.

There was no one in sight and it was growing dark. I climbed over the rail, held my breath and made the leap. The window went up easily and no one cracked me in the head, but it wasn't doing my new suit any good.

I pulled myself into a small bathroom and got to my feet as soon as I could. No one came rushing into the room, and I could see beyond the open door that the lights were out.

Beaumont might be waiting for me. I looked for a weapon and settled on a jar of Molle shaving cream. The apartment was empty. Beaumont wasn't under the bed or in a closet. I had either missed him in the hall or he had grabbed something and ran down the fire escape.

It was a nice apartment, three rooms with maid service. It didn't even look lived in. I turned the lights on and searched. It was an easy place to search, but it took time. I was checking everything. Beaumont may have made it down the fire escape with my gun, Adelman's money and the negative, but he might have left one or all of them here. On the other hand, he might never have had any of them.

Fifteen minutes later I had found nothing. I was looking under the rolled up carpet when I heard footsteps in the hall. I started to get up when the door opened and a gun came through.

I was on my knees. It seemed a bad way to go, and Beaumont had every legal right to put a few bullets in my face. I was breaking and entering. There was nothing within reach to throw.

The gun that came through the door was attached to an arm which was attached to a familiar body and face.

Three men walked in.

"You gonna sing Mammy?" asked the man with the gun.

I got off my knees. The man with the gun was my brother. Seidman was behind him followed by the clerk from downstairs.

"That's him," said the clerk with a pleased grin. He looked as if he wanted to jump up and down with excitement. "Said he was a homicide detective and showed me that fake badge." He sneered at me with his pimpled face. "Didn't fool me for a second. I called Mr. Simmons right away and warned him. Probably saved his life."

"You did a fine job, Mr. Plautt," said Seidman. "Now don't you think you should get back to your desk?"

"He tried to talk to me about Baby Snooks, . . ." Plautt continued, but Phil interrupted him through his teeth.

"Go downstairs, Mr. Plautt."

Plautt gave me another look and went down the hall. We could hear him pause and shout back:

"If there's a reward, I get it."

Phil slammed the door.

"You couldn't even fool that half wit," my brother said, flopping into a chair. Seidman leaned against the wall and folded his hands.

"Get off your knees, you asshole," shouted Phil.

I got up putting my tale together.

"Listen, Phil, I . . ."

"No story, Toby, none, just answers. This guy Simmons has you on breaking and entering as soon as we find him. I've got you on impersonating a policeman."

"I didn't impersonate a policeman," I said. "I simply told the guy two words: 'homicide' and 'Pevsner.' I am investigating a homicide and my name is Pevsner. I showed him a private investigator's badge."

Phil rubbed a big hand over his tired face and put his gun away. "That is the dumbest defense I've ever heard."

"You gave the impression that you were a police officer," said Seidman. "That's the same thing as identifying yourself as one."

"Who's Simmons?" asked Phil softly, his head coming up from his hand. Phil was most dangerous when he talked softly.

"He may be the guy who killed Cunningham," I said. "I got a tip and followed him here."

"Why didn't you call us?" said Phil.

I walked over to where he was sitting and kept talking.

"No time. I don't think Simmons is his real name, and I don't think he'll be back here. When that jerk desk clerk called him, I think Simmons took off with the gun he used to kill Cunningham." I left out the possibility of the negative and the $5,000. I wasn't too sure about the gun either.

My eyes were fixed on Phil's to see how much of this he was taking in, and how much he believed. He tooked tired and let out a massive sigh before the back of his hand came up and caught me on the side of the head. I was moving away from it when it hit me. I had been half expecting it. I staggered a few feet, bounced off a wall and tasted blood. Seidman looked on emotionlessly.

"Let's go," said Phil, pulling himself up from the chair. I followed him out the door, and Seidman went behind me. There was no blood on my new suit. Phil handed me a handkerchief over his shoulder, and I put it against my mouth.

"You mind if we just leave my car in the lot around the corner," I said. "I've already picked up two tickets in front of police headquarters."

As we went through the lobby, Plautt, the desk clerk, grinned happily.

"So you see, Sergeant," I said back to Seidman, loud enough for the clerk to hear, "I couldn't reveal myself as an F.B.I. agent, not where Nazi spies were involved."

I thought I caught a slight smile on Seidman's face. Plautt's jaw dropped.

Seidman drove through neon streets, and I sat in back of the unmarked car with Phil. Phil said only one thing and then looked out the window.

"We picked up one of the guys who broke into your place, Fagin. We want you to make a positive identification and file charges."

"Then you're not arresting me for breaking into Simmons' place and impersonating an officer?"

"Drop it, Peters," Seidman said, from the front seat.

I shut up. It was nice to be driven somewhere for a change.

The man who looked like a mailbox was sitting in Phil's office, guarded by a uniformed cop. Fagin and the cop were in a hot discussion about whether L.A. could support a pro football team. Fagin said yes, the cop, no.

"Is that the man who broke into your apartment last night and tried to kill you?" said Phil, pointing at the mailbox.

Fagin, his bald head gleaming and his neck invisible, tried to look innocent, but the blank look only made him appear more stupid. Without much work, he could find a good defense in mental incompetence.

"I think so," I said.

Both Seidman and Phil looked at me.

"Could I talk to him alone?" I said.

"Hello no," shouted Phil. "What the hell do you want to talk to him alone about?"

"In that case," I said, "I'd have to say that's not one of the men."

Fagin was confused and looking more stupid by the second. He knew he was the man, and so did everyone else in the room with the possible exception of the uniformed cop.

"O.K., Toby," said Phil, "you have five minutes." He jerked his head toward the door. Seidman and the uniformed cop followed him out of the door and closed it.

I looked at Fagin.

"I'm not the guy you're looking for, buddy," he said. "I was home sleeping when those guys took you. Honest."

I sat on the edge of my brother's desk and grinned down at Fagin.

"It was you, and I'm going to see that you get nailed for it," I said, sounding tough and cynical.

Fagin's attempt at honesty turned quickly to animal attack.

"I've got two terms against me in Folsom," said Fagin; "if I go up to Quentin or the Rock for this, I'll see to it that someone makes you sorry you were born."

He may have meant it, and he may have been bluffing. The odds were even that if I sent him up, I'd get a knife or bullet in the back some night. I was willing to risk it, but I had some other ideas.

"I've been threatened by bigger tuna than you, sport," I said, "but we might be able to work something out."

He sat forward in his chair eagerly, a solid Humpty Dumpty.

"Who hired you to get me and why?"

"Delamater hired me," he said. "That's all I know. I don't even know what he wanted from you. I was just hired muscle. It sounded like an easy job. He didn't think we'd have to kill you. I didn't want to kill you."

"You're all heart," I said. "What did Delamater tell you about me, the job, anything?"

"Nothing." He was sweating.

"You give me nothing. I give you nothing," I said, forcing my eyes to keep from blinking.

"Yeah," he growled.

"Yeah," I growled back. He would barely qualify for cretin of the year, but he was all I had to work with. "Tell me what he told you."

Fagin wiped his sweating forehead with his sleeve and tried to think. It was a major effort.

"He said we were going to a guy's place and throw a scare into him. That we might have to hurt him bad if he didn't give us something we were looking for."

"What?"

"Some kind of picture," said Fagin. "But," he went on, excited, "he said we didn't want killing, for sure. He said she doesn't want the guy killed, that's you, unless we have to. That . . ."

"Hold it." I put my hand on his arm, and he jumped. Concentrating on the story had taken all of his attention. "You said 'she'?"

"Right," said Fagin. "She, Delamater said 'she'. We were doing the job for some woman, but he didn't give her name or anything. Told us the pay was good."

I walked to the door and called Phil in.

He and Seidman were drinking coffee.

Fagin looked up in fear.

"That's not the man," I said.

Fagin's shit-eating grin filled the room.

"You son-of-a-bitch," said Phil, shaking his head. Then to Fagin, "Get out before I get some Flit and use it on you."

Fagin simply sat grinning.

"He means get out of here," I said.

"Right, sure, thanks," he beamed, plunked on a hat that came down to his ears, and went out the door.

"I don't know what you're playing, Toby," Phil grunted wearily, "but I don't like being used. That creep was the right one, and we all know it. What did you get out of him?"

"I'm not under arrest?"

"Not unless we find Simmons, and he brings charges," said Phil, his hands folded. He was giving me a look of resignation.

"That wasn't the right guy, Phil. I swear . . ."

"Get out." His voice was so low I could hardly hear it.

"Look, Phil . . ." I started.

"You better go," said Seidman, opening the door. I went.

At the corner drug store where I had been earlier that morning, I had a Pepsi and a Pecan Roll. Then I called Brenda Beaumont. The maid said she was busy. I said to tell her I had just talked to a friend of Mr. Delamater.

Brenda Beaumont was on the phone about a minute later.

"What do you want, Mr. Peters?" she said, as if I were interrupting her with a request for an autograph.

"Not what you were selling the other day," I said. "I've got questions. Either you answer them for me or I give the whole mess to the Los Angeles police, and they can ask you. Like what was your husband talking to you about when he visited you this afternoon? Why did you try to have me messed up? And the best one, who killed Charlie Cunningham? Are you listening, Brenda?"

"I'm listening. I can't talk now, tonight. Can you come over tomorrow night, about nine. I'll tell you everything I know; but please don't go to the police, for Lynn, if not for me."

"Tomorrow night at nine, sharp," I said. "You going to offer me your body or a fat bankroll again?" I was angry.

"Would it do any good?"

"None," I said. I hung up.

By the time I got a yellow cab and picked up my car near Beaumont's apartment, it was getting late. I should have called Adelman, but I was tired. I decided not to go to what was left of my apartment. My reasons weren't aesthetic. Brenda Beaumont might have other friends, and my apartment was turning into a casting room for a gangster movie.

I knew where I wanted to go and headed there. It took me about half an hour to get to the apartment building in Culver City. I had the address memorized and found the place without any trouble. The name over the doorbell gave me a burst of youthful anticipation. At least that's what I told myself. The feeling was more like vague hope.

Looking firmly at the name "Ann Peters" in white letters against a black background, I pressed the button and heard a soft chime bong somewhere inside the building. It was a freshly-built, elongated two-story white antiseptic building with cheap, but pleasant smelling carpets. I thought about pulling myself together, straightening my tie and forcing a smile.

No one answered the bell. I tried again and a buzzer sounded. I pulled the lobby door open just as the buzzing stopped and I stood for a second, my knees feeling weak. As I went up to the second floor, my tactics changed. Helplessness seemed a more likely key to success. I could see a door open at the end of the short corridor on the second floor and was sure about my tactics:

Ann stepped out in the hall and watched me as I approached. She had done something truly unfair since our divorce. She looked better. During some of our fights, I had warned her that she would go to fat when she hit 40, just like her mother, who could hardly walk because of the hereditary load she carried. Ann had always been full and dark and she had been hurt by the suggestion, because it was probably true. She had always fought back at me with a series of good ones about money, ambition, family.

I stood in front of her in the hallway. She was thinner than she had been when I saw her three years earlier. She didn't just look better with her hair long and down and a clinging blue robe; she looked great.

"Hi," I said with a smile.

Her hands were folded and she held her arms close to her body, unsure for a second of how to deal with me. Her frown softened.

"Toby, you look awful." She stepped back and made it clear that I could enter her apartment.

"Thanks," I said stepping in, "I was hoping for that. I had considered a 'Hell, I'm going great,' run down the hall, but I took the pathetic cat ploy instead."

She shook her head and sighed. It made her breasts rise and my hopes with them.

"Toby," she said looking at my face, "You didn't have a choice.

You'd look pathetic with a new suit, a shave and a smile. What happened to you?"

I looked around the room, deciding on my next move, knowing that she was at least a step ahead. The room was furnished in modern brown chairs and sofas, really one of each. The carpet was a light brown and the wallpaper was a tasteful brown and white. A painting of two factory workers shaking hands was on one wall. I walked over to it, pretending to admire it, waiting for Ann to carry the load.

"Toby, I'll ask once more. What happened to you? Make it reasonably short, because the next question is, what are you doing here?"

I examined her sadly and sat, uninvited, on the sofa. It was firm. I expected it to be, everything about Ann was firm, from her ideas to her thighs. In the beginning we thought the combination of daydreamer and realist was a good one. We both gave each other something the other one needed. But as time went on, I gave her fewer dreams and her realism depressed me.

"Ann, I have been beaten, shot at, beaten again, threatened and ridiculed," I said looking at the floor. "Someone may be planning to kill me and there's a good chance I'll be arrested for murder."

My eyes moved up to her face which was filled with amusement but not sympathy.

"Great," she said, "then you must be having a fine time. It sounds like what you always wanted. I'll get you a cup of coffee. I'm sorry, but I don't have any cereal." She left the room through a white door leading, I guessed, to the kitchen.

When she was gone, I smiled to myself. She was right. I was really enjoying the whole thing and I'd probably come to let her know just that. Well, I'd come with other things in mind too.

"You seem to be doing all right," I said raising my voice. "I'm glad you didn't need the alimony."

Her laugh bounced off of the walls and hit between my eyes.

"Toby, you haven't put together enough money in your whole life to make the alimony payment for an impoverished cleaning lady." Her voice sounded neither bitter nor angry as she spoke. "Trying to get alimony out of you would have taken more effort than going to work."

"You're still at the airline?"

"Yes," she said returning to the room with two cups of coffee. As she handed me one and sat down with the other, her robe opened a little at the top. She saw me looking and sat back with her cup shaking her head.

"You're the same, Toby. You'll be the same when you're 70 if you live that long."

I took some coffee. It was hot. She must have had the coffee brewing when I came.

"You still use the name Ann Peters," I said, my eyes fixed on her face.

"I have the legal right to it," she said quietly and confidently.

"Oh," I said holding up a hand, "you're welcome to it. It's a link between us."

"No, it's not. Peters isn't even your real name. Now if I were to go back to my maiden name, it would be a liability in my work."

"What's wrong with Ann Mitzenmacher?" I said enjoying the old back-and-forth with her.

Her face went serious as she drained her cup and rose.

"There's nothing wrong with Ann Mitzenmacher," she whispered, "which is why I'm going to have to ask you to finish your coffee, accept my sympathy and leave."

I finished the coffee and got up.

"Annie . . ." I stopped because a frown from the past came to her face. "I'm sorry," I continued, "Ann, I need a place to stay tonight."

Her head was making a slight 'no' motion and her lower lip came out in an ironic pout.

"No, Toby. Not tonight, not any night."

"Ann," I said stepping toward her, "I promise, no monkey business, just some talk about old times and I go to sleep on that sofa." I crossed my heart.

"Toby, I'm expecting company," she said.

"Oh," I replied looking for a next move and finding none in my body or on my tongue. "A gentleman caller?"

Her head said yes.

"It's none of your business," she said gently, "but this is a special gentleman caller. My apartment is not an orgy center."

"You work with him?" I asked.

"I work with him," she answered, "and I am sorry you came tonight. I didn't invite you. If it helps, I do feel sorry for you, but not for the reasons you'd like. You don't want to grow up, Toby. You never did."

"True and not true," I said. "Not true because . . ."

"No," she said walking to the door. "I don't want to hear."

I went slowly and quietly to the door. Defeat was total and the consolation was a soft kiss Ann gave me. I tried to turn the kiss into something, but she pulled back and opened the door.

"Goodbye Toby," she said.

"I'll see you," I tried.

"I hope not," were her last words as the door closed behind me.

As I went down the hall slowly on the chance that the door would open behind me, I heard the chime ring in her apartment. Going down the carpeted stairway, I heard the lobby door open. A man passed me as I hit the bottom step. He was about 50, very well dressed with neat grey hair. I couldn't tell for sure if he was in good shape, wearing a corset or just holding his stomach in. All three possibilities made me tired.

I got in my Buick and headed for my office. The building was dark when I arrived. As quietly as I could, I went up the stairs, through the office door, past the reception room and into the dental chair. I took off my tie and jacket in the dark, lowered Sheldon's dental chair and closed my eyes. The phone rang once, but I ignored it. In a few minutes, I was asleep. This time I had no dream.

11

MY EYES OPENED TO MORNING and a horrible sight, D.D.S. Shelly Minck's face, complete with cigar and glasses inches from mine.

"I thought you were dead or something," said Shelly.

"Not yet," I got up.

He gathered his tools together and put on some coffee while we talked and I shaved.

"Four big ones today," Shelly gloated, taking his cigar out of his mouth to wash his hands. "An extraction, some bridgework and two patients with fillings. Business is picking up I tell you, Toby. The Depression is over. F.D.R. is getting my vote."

"Glad to hear it, Shelly." I fixed my tie, took one of Shelly's sample toothbrushes and scrubbed my teeth.

After a breakfast of coffee and sweet rolls, I headed for Warner Brothers. It was a clear, bright day, and I had the feeling that I was close to a lot of answers. My immediate goal was to try to talk Adelman out of $200 and get a line on Beaumont.

Hatch wasn't on the gate. The guy who was, was scrawny and mean and didn't know me. He said Hatch was around, but he wasn't about to look for him. He called Adelman's office.

The scrawny guard got the O.K. from Adelman and passed me through.

When I entered the building, Adelman was standing in front of his office. He was trying to calm an excited, thin man of about fifty.

"That explains nothink, nothink Sidney, nothink." The man's accent was thick and European, and he was angry.

"Mike," said Adelman reasonably, "what am I asking? A day? You can shoot around him for a day?"

"I shot around one day of him," said Mike. "Enough. Tomorrow he returns or I talk to Jack Warner. I have an empty horse where Flynn should be, Sidney."

Sid shook his head in sympathy.

"I know that, Mike," he said. "Believe me, I know. Check back with me later, I'll do what I can."

"What you can," said Mike, glancing at me as I advanced, "is to get him back tomorrow on the morning."

The man walked past me, and Sid looked after him shaking his head.

"That's Mike Curtiz," said Sid seeing me. "He's directing *Santa Fe Trail,* the picture Flynn is supposed to be on. You heard. He wants him back. Jesus. Come in. Come in." Sid ushered me past Esther, who didn't look up, and into his office.

Bill Faulkner wasn't at home. Sid parked himself behind his desk and started to fidget with his pens and pencils.

"You owe me two hundred dollars," I said sitting.

"You've got the negative and my money back?"

"No, but I found the girl in the picture. She doesn't know Flynn, and he doesn't know her. The picture is a fake."

"You can prove it?" said Adelman eagerly.

"If we have to, with a doctor. The girl's a virgin."

"Virgin?"

"Yes," I said. "So, if your blackmailer calls, we'll work out something to trap him."

"Who's the girl?" said Adelman, gazing at the photo of Roosevelt.

"She stays out of this," I said. "She didn't know what was happening. Cunningham drugged her and faked the picture. Now about my two hundred dollars."

"No negative, no cash, no two hundred," said Adelman. He actually rubbed his hands together. "Now we can get Flynn back here. Curtiz will get off my back and . . ."

"Hold on, Sid. I still don't know who killed Cunningham and who tried to kill Flynn. Whoever it is may make another try at Flynn."

"We'll give him protection," he shouted, adjusting his tie. "I'll send a couple of studio security men to watch him. Where is he?"

I told him and said the next step was finding Harry Beaumont.

"Why? What's the klutz got to do with this?"

"I don't know, but I've got to ask him some questions."

"So go ask him," Sid said standing. "He's doing a short over on the back lot."

I went for the door before Sid could say anything more.

"Esther, you look beautiful," I shouted. "A double for Constance Bennett."

The back lot at Warner Brothers was a series of exterior sets that ran into each other. There was a fake city street that could be anything from Chicago to London. There was a Western street right around the corner and a fake tenement block a little further on. Shooting was going on on every set. At the edge of the lot, in a corner, I spotted the deck of a pirate ship. A camera crew was shooting two men on the deck. The two men were sword fighting. One of the men was a little comedian whose name I couldn't remember. The man he was fighting with was Harry Beaumont.

I came up to the group slowly, trying to stay out of the line of Beaumont's vision. Beaumont was wearing a pirate costume including a bandana and red-and-white striped shirt. He looked mean. When the director called out, Beaumont added a sullen look to the mean one.

"Come on, Harry," the director shouted, "put some life into the shot."

"You've got all the life you're getting out of me for a lousy two-reel comedy," Beaumont answered angrily. "I'm not doing another take."

"We haven't got the budget for another take," said the director, who shared sympathetic looks with the little comedian and called a break.

Beaumont was clearly on the way down. Last year, second leads in A pictures and a few leads in B's; this year, the villain in a two-reel comedy. Next year, a character actor in summer theater in Fresno. Beaumont moved alone to the rail on the ship and leaned over to look at the sky and mountains. The crew wandered away.

As quietly as I could, I moved behind Beaumont and then next to him at the rail.

"Future doesn't look too good does it, Harry?"

He turned to me suddenly, but I was ready and had my arms loosely at my side.

"Harry," I whispered, "we can talk quietly or fight. I'd rather fight."

"What do you want?"

"Did you kill Charlie Cunningham?"

The hatred in his eyes was no act. I was threatening what little he had going for him, and he wasn't about to give it up easily.

"I didn't kill Cunningham."

"Can you prove that?"

"Yes," he said with a twisted smile. "At two in the morning yesterday I was with a young lady who will be happy to testify to that effect."

"Who said he was killed at two," I asked.

Maybe he was starting to sweat from the question. Maybe it was just the aftermath of the fake fight with the comic.

"You told Brenda, my wife, and I saw her yesterday. She told me."

He had been to see his wife. I was his witness for that, but I couldn't remember whether I had told her when Cunningham was killed. I didn't think I had.

"Next question," I went on, "when you stopped at the apartment you're renting under the name of Simmons, did you pick up something and take it with you?"

"Like . . ."

"A gun, a negative of your daughter and Errol Flynn, five thousand dollars," I said.

"No," he said, looking away. He played bored, but I wasn't buying it.

"Then you won't mind my searching your clothes and having a look in that Caddy you drive?"

That did it.

"If you wish," he said, turning slowly, as if he had all the time in the world. It was the same turn he had made in the farm at Buellton. His repertoire was limited. He turned fast with something in his hand and swung it at me. I ducked and came in with a hard left just below his ribs. It felt good, but he didn't go down. Instead, he hit me in the shoulder with the block of wood he had lifted from the rail. I came back with a right to the side of his head that made one of my knuckles pop and swell.

Beaumont grunted and ran at me. His head caught me in the chest, throwing me backward.

The crew for the short was moving toward us. A few of the people, including the director, cheered me on. Beaumont turned and ran.

In the next few minutes, we destroyed a lot of good footage and confused some of the best talent in Hollywood.

A troop of soldiers was marching down a muddy street. Beaumont plowed into them, and someone screamed "cut"! I followed Beaumont through the mud. End of new suit and last pair of shoes.

The soldiers stopped and watched while Beaumont panted his way around a corner. I was about twenty yards behind him. When I turned the corner, he was gone. I hurried down the space between the two buildings where he disappeared and found a door. The shooting light was on, but I went in. I heard familiar voices in the darkness and made my way through the shadows toward the light of the set. Beaumont was standing among extras looking over his shoulder for me. He stood out like a pirate among tuxedoed politicians, which is exactly what he was.

He spotted me stepping into the light and turned to run, but his path was blocked by the extras. I started after him, and he ran right into the set.

It was a fancy home. Edward Arnold was behind a desk wearing a tux. Gary Cooper, wearing a rumpled suit, was carrying on a conversation with him.

Just as Arnold said, "Listen here, Doe" to Cooper, Beaumont started across the set. I went over an assistant director's back and tackled Beaumont, who thudded against the desk knocking it and Arnold over. I didn't see what happened to Cooper.

Beaumont had turned and had his fingers around my neck. I butted him with my head and punched him with my left hand. The right one throbbed from the earlier punch.

Somewhere behind me somebody said, "Should we cut, Mr. Capra?"

"Hell no," came a delighted voice.

I was getting tired, but Beaumont must have been in worse shape. He rolled over on me. His weight was his main advantage. My head hit something, and Beaumont was off me and moving again. I could hear him puffing.

Someone helped me up. It was Gary Cooper.

"Thanks," I breathed.

"My pleasure," he said, lifting his eyebrow.

Beaumont was out of another door, and I was behind him. He pushed a couple of girls in cheerleaders' uniforms and went through another door. We were on the Knute Rockne gym set where I had played table tennis with Don Siegel.

We moved slowly, very slowly, and Beaumont almost collapsed.

His back against the bleachers, he turned for a goal line stand. A weak right came up, and then he made a grab for me with his arms wide. I stepped back and hit him in the face with a right. It hurt like hell, but I felt his bone crack, and he went down.

I was exhausted and breathing hard. I sat on the floor and started to go through his pockets. He wasn't unconscious, but there wasn't enough left in him to raise his arms. It was in the back pocket of his pants under his pirate suit. The envelope was small, brown, big enough to hold a four by five negative. I opened it and recognized the negative. It was the same one I had held in my hand a few seconds before Cunningham was killed.

I started to put the picture in my jacket pocket and pull myself up. Beaumont, his nose bloody, looked up at me. He looked frightened and gulped blood.

"You're really something, Harry," I gasped. "Using pictures of your own daughter for blackmail. I've seen them low, but not as low as you are right now."

His eyes looked up at me pleading, but they weren't focusing properly. Then I realized that they weren't focusing on me. It was like the moment just before Cunningham caught the bullet from my gun. I started to turn toward where Beaumont was looking. Something inside, maybe experience, told me to duck when I turned. It probably saved my life. There was an explosion, and I saw the inkwell in my desk when I was a kid in third grade. I dived into the ink and swam lazily in the darkness. It was pleasant. After a while I came out of the ink and opened my eyes. I had a feeling that I was alive, but might wish I wasn't.

The negative was gone. I knew it would be. Beaumont was still there. I was afraid he would be. His eyes were wide open, and there were two red holes through the chest of the pirate uniform.

For a minute or two, I sat in the middle of the gymnasium set with my third corpse in two days. This one was the worst. Half of the Warner Brothers lot had seen me fighting with Beaumont. It was even on film, and here I sat with his body. I would have bet my car, my salary from Flynn and the two hundred I would probably never collect from Adelman that the two bullets in Beaumont's chest were from my gun.

If history was repeating itself, someone would be coming in a few minutes, and it would probably be the cops. They were getting less friendly with me with each encounter.

My head was sore. I touched it and felt blood. The killer had tried to make it three, but I was a secondary target, and the bullet had only plowed a furrow in my scalp. The gun wasn't in sight.

I didn't expect it to be. I got up, looked at Beaumont once more, and moved into the darkness of the set. There were no sirens, and I heard no footsteps, but it wouldn't be long before my brother was after me. This time, I was sure, he wouldn't let me walk out of his office.

I found a water tap outside the building and stuck my head under it. I splashed some water on my muddy legs and shoes, pulled myself together and stumbled in the general direction of my car. I was going to be lucky to come out of this whole thing with my brains still unscrambled.

When I turned the corner in front of Sid's office, I saw my car. Seidman was standing next to it. My brother was probably inside talking to Adelman about Cunningham. In a few seconds, my brother would know about me and Beaumont and follow my trail through ruined footage. I headed away from my car and toward the front gate.

I walked out of the gate as briskly as I could and caught a Sunshine cab which had just dropped someone off. I told the Italian driver to take me to the Y.

"You a movie actor or writer or something?" he asked.

"No," I said, "but I've got something to do with pictures."

"I just gave a ride to a producer named Blanke," said the driver, "you heard of him?"

"Yeah," I said, trying to decide what I was going to do until nine o'clock.

"Cheap. Quarter tip," said the cabbie.

"Well," I said closing my eyes, "you just never know what to expect from these movie people."

12

THE CABBIE DROPPED ME OFF in front of the Y, but I decided not to stay there. My brother might check cabs leaving the studio and give my description. That might lead to the Y.M.C.A. Phil would figure me to be smarter than that, but he'd check it out anyway.

I walked a few blocks, got another cab and went three blocks past a cheap hotel I knew on San Pedro. I had once spent the night at the place talking a runaway grandmother into going home to her son and daughter-in-law. The old lady had been living happily in the hotel when I found her. Her son was the owner of a pretty big Van Nuys toy store, and he paid cash up front. I remembered the hotel had asked her no questions and had been surprisingly clean.

I registered as Murray Sklar. When amateurs register anonymously, they usually keep some part of their real name, maybe the same initials, or their middle name. I moved as far as I could from mine. I had no luggage, but I paid cash, and the woman at the desk appreciated being compared to Joan Crawford. Most of the women in Los Angeles thought they looked like Jean Harlow, Joan Crawford, Joan Blondell or Olivia DeHavilland. The Joan Crawford behind the desk looked more like Marjorie Main in *Dead End*.

The room was clean and neat, but small. I didn't care. I only expected to stay for a few hours. There was a phone in the hall. I called Sid Adelman.

"What the hell are you doing? Just what the hell are you doing?" he huffed. "I'll tell you what you're doing. You're killing off the goddamn employees of this studio one by one."

"I didn't kill them, Sid, and besides, you really won't miss any of them."

"That's not the point," he cried. "The publicity is going to be terrible, terrible if anyone finds out. We may be able to keep it out of the papers, but I don't know." Long pause. "Was Beaumont the second blackmailer?"

"I think so," I said. An old man in a bathrobe passed by me in the hall. I nodded and spoke more softly. "I had my hands on the negative for a few seconds again."

"And you lost it, huh putz?" I could imagine Sid Adelman shaking his little head.

A relatively old lady of the evening walked past me down the hall. She didn't look as good as Marjorie Main in *Dead End*. I gave her a polite smile and shrugged at the phone indicating I was too busy.

"What did the cops want?" I asked Adelman.

"Bette Davis's autograph," he said sarcastically. "They wanted you. They want you. Some lieutenant named Pevsner will probably kill you if he gets his hands on you."

"So they know about me fighting with Beaumont?"

"And," he dripped, "ruining several hundred feet of film and destroying one short comedy by killing the villain."

"Sidney, I didn't kill him."

"The cops think it was you. I'm supposed to tell you to call Lieutenant Pevsner if you call me. Call Lieutenant Pevsner. There, I told you."

I asked him if he had sent someone to guard Flynn at the hotel. The killer was obviously someone who could get onto the lot without trouble. If he could get on the lot, he might have no trouble finding Flynn in the hotel. Flynn was not doing a good job of keeping his hiding place secret.

"I'm not a jerk, Peters," he said wearily. "Two of our best security men have been with him since we talked. Whannel and Ellis. You know them?"

"Good men," I said.

"And tonight," he went on, "Hatch and Kindem take over at midnight when they've finished their shift. You know them?"

"Hatch is a good man. I don't know the other guy. Sounds fine, Sid."

He thanked me nastily for my approval and told me to call when I had a killer in hand. Flynn was still holding up production on *Santa Fe Trail.* He had a big scene scheduled for the next day with Raymond Massey. I said I'd do my best. He hung up.

I went down to the desk and asked Marjorie Main if I could get my suit cleaned and pressed and my shoes taken care of. I gave her all my gleaming teeth, and she blushed.

Fifteen minutes later an elderly kid came to my room and took my clothes and shoes. It would cost me fifteen bucks, he said. I told him it was fine and lay in bed listening to the radio.

On KFI, Jimmy Fiddler told me that Vivien Leigh and Laurence Olivier were just married and Humphrey Bogart's career was skyrocketing.

H.V. Kaltenborn said there was good news: that we were almost certain to stay out of the European war, and that prosperity had returned. For about twenty minutes I listened to Sammy Kaye and his orchestra playing from the Make Believe Ballroom. Then there was a knock on the door. It was the elderly kid. He had my clothes. I gave him the fifteen bucks, and he waited for a tip. I knew he was keeping at least five anyway, but I was in no position to upset him. I flipped him two halves. What the hell. I was going to charge it to Errol Flynn for expenses, and he could afford it.

My suit was reasonably clean, and my shoes looked fine. I got dressed and went to the hall to call Flynn. He answered.

"Toby, there have been three more attempts on my life," he said.

Tension ran through me.

"What happened?"

"Three women caught me in the hall and tried to tear me apart in ecstasy," he said with a sigh.

"Very funny, Errol. Are the guards there from the studio?"

"Yes," he said, "but I don't like it. Bruce and Guinn went home and the two gentlemen are with me now. Toby, I don't like being treated as if I were some delicacy. Tomorrow morning I am going back to work."

"But . . ." I began.

"Jack Warner does not think me a particularly good actor," he said soberly. "In some respects I agree with him though I am improving, and a few people like Raoul Walsh keep telling me I'm good. In any case, I've at least been reliable."

"Harry Beaumont was murdered this afternoon," I tried. "It was probably by the same guy who killed Cunningham and tried to kill you."

"Yes," he said, "I'm well aware of all that, but tomorrow morning I will leave here, go to the studio, put on my cavalry uniform and join Ronald Reagan in confronting Raymond Massey in the guise of John Brown. Right now I am going to have a small drink with Mr. Whannel and Ellis from the studio and excuse myself to entertain a lady. Take care, Toby," he said sincerely and hung up.

He was certainly likeable even if he wasn't the most reasonable person I had ever met.

It was 7:30. I decided to visit Brenda Beaumont an hour or so earlier than she had invited me. It might be much safer that way. There was nothing for me to pack. I left the key at the desk with the woman and said I didn't know what time I would be back. She said goodby, Mr. Sklar.

A few minutes later I was in a Black and White cab on the way to Beverly Hills. Black and White cabs were "confined to Negro districts" according to the Chamber of Commerce. But the Negro drivers sometimes took a chance. I gave the driver an address a block away from the Beaumont house. I didn't know if there was such an address. The driver was quiet, and that was the way I liked it.

He stopped at a big house in Beverly Hills about fifteen minutes later. The address was wrong, but I said it was the right house. I overtipped him and crossed the road walking in the twilight toward the Beaumont house. If it was being watched or guarded, I wanted to know.

For ten minutes, I stood quietly under a tree. It looked all right. There were a few lights on downstairs and one or two upstairs.

I went all the way around the big street to the back of the house and found the gate where Brenda Beaumont had tried to get me out during my other visit. The pool house was a fifteen foot run from the gate. I hoped the door was open. There was a light on near the pool, but no one was swimming. The lock on the gate was good, but old. I backed away and gave it a kick. From the front of the house I could hear Jamie and Ralph barking. Their barks got close faster. Dogs from nearby homes joined in the noise. I pushed the gate open.

I ran for the pool house and was a foot from the door just as the two pincers came around the edge of the pool house. I caught only a glimpse of them as I hit the door and went in. I kicked the door closed with my foot and almost caught one of the dogs in the snout. By the outside light I went to the front door. I took a deep breath, opened it a crack and went to the rear door, where the dogs were barking and clawing. I put a chair lightly against the door and ran for the front door. The dogs leaped in pushing the chair away as they sprang. They couldn't have been more than three feet behind me when I went through the front door and closed it.

Without stopping, I ran around the pool house toward the back door. I didn't know how smart Dobermans were, but I hoped I was a step or two smarter. When I got to the back door, they had just figured the whole thing out and were dashing back toward me. I slammed the back door and leaned against the wall trembling.

I had them trapped in the pool house, and they were none too happy about it.

Moving to the pool, I stood and looked at the house for a few minutes. Nothing moved. Maybe Jamie and Ralph were frequent noisemakers. Since they were still barking, the people in the house probably thought they were all right, and things were in hand. At least, that's what I was hoping for.

As it turned out, I was wrong. I was greeted at the back door leading from the living room to the garden by Brenda Beaumont. She was wearing black, a black suit and a small, black gun. She fit the room perfectly as she turned on the lights. She looked beautiful.

"Mr. Peters, you're early."

"I was in the neighborhood," I said. "But I can come back later if it's a bad time. I don't want to disturb you and Lynn and the maid."

"Lynn is staying overnight at a friend's, and Juanita has the night off. We are quite alone," she said grimly.

"Very romantic."

"You are not charming," she said leveling the gun at me. "Now you will give me the picture you have of Lynn."

I took my wallet out carefully and handed her the picture of the girl.

"All this isn't necessary," I said. "In the first place, someone has the negative and can turn out hundreds of pictures."

"I know who has the negative," she said, "and it won't be used to hurt Lynn or anyone else. It will be destroyed."

"That makes things a little difficult," I said. "The person who has that negative killed your husband this afternoon."

"The police have already been here," she said, sitting carefully, taking a cigarette and reaching for the Oscar lighter. She was trying to get up enough courage to do something, and I didn't like what I thought it might be.

"Lynn's a nice kid," I said.

"I don't need your opinion." The gun came up, and I held my hands in front of me.

"Wait a minute," I said amiably, "it's not going to do her much good to have her father dead and her mother on trial for murder."

"I won't be on trial for murder," she said. "We're going up to my room. We are going to throw a few things around so it will look as if we had a struggle. You came here demanding money."

"For what?" I said. "You're not going to get Lynn involved."

"No, but I have a very nice print of the picture of me and Charlie Cunningham. The police, I understand, know you were at his apartment. They will find the picture on you."

She motioned me up the stairs inside the house. I walked five feet in front of her, trying to decide when to make my move.

She turned lights on ahead of us and guided me at gunpoint into her bedroom. It was nice, soft and white with fur all around.

"How about some answers before you shoot me," I said.

"I don't plan to *shoot* you unless I have to."

"Glad to hear that," I smiled, but I didn't ask what she planned to do. "First, you hired Delamater to get Lynn's picture from me, right?"

"Right," she said, knocking everything but a framed photograph from her dressing table, while keeping the gun leveled at me. "I remembered him from the studio and that he had been in trouble. Charlie also knew him vaguely. Next question." She moved across the room carefully and turned over a chair. She was lying about Delamater, but I couldn't figure her angle.

"Why did your husband visit you yesterday?"

She shook her blonde hair, and I could see her reflected endlessly in mirrors opposite each other on the wall. She was a spot of silken black and gold in total whiteness.

"He wanted me to pay him for the negative of Lynn," she said.

"Nice man," I said.

She hurled a perfume bottle at one of the mirrors, shattering pieces around the room. I covered my head.

"Did you pay?" I asked.

"I said I would," she whispered, looking around the room for something else to break.

"But, instead you told somebody," I guessed. "Somebody who

knew where to find Harry, went to the studio, killed him and took the negative, right?"

She looked weak and pale. If my life weren't on the line, I would have felt sorry for her.

"He . . . Harry wouldn't give up the negative," she said so softly that I almost missed it.

"So, the same person who killed Cunningham killed Harry," I went on, looking for something to throw or a light switch I could hit. "In both cases, they were killed to keep the negative of Lynn from being used for blackmail."

She nodded. Peter Lorre had been dead right. I'd have to look him up and tell him if I survived.

"Brenda, didn't you know that photograph was a fake?"

She looked at me suspiciously.

"It's a fake and we can prove it. All you had to do was ask Lynn, your own daughter." I walked slowly toward her. "Don't you even talk to her?"

The gun lowered slightly, uncertainly, as she spoke.

"We . . . we don't talk much, especially not about . . ."

"You thought it was real?" I was a few feet from her. "You and whoever committed two murders weren't close enough to Lynn to even talk to her."

"She, she doesn't trust me," Brenda Beaumont almost cried. "She knew about Charlie and me, and others. I thought Charlie had gotten to her. I knew how . . . how charming he could be."

The gun was aiming at the floor, and I was a few feet from her. I glanced around the room without moving my head. Then I saw it. My eyes focused on the photograph on her dressing table. It was the only thing still standing on it, a picture of Brenda, Harry, Lynn and a man, in better days. It was obviously a family portrait. The whole thing was suddenly clear to me. I knew who had killed Charlie Cunningham, taken a shot at Flynn and murdered Harry Beaumont.

Brenda looked up and saw my eyes. She followed them to the

picture and knew that I knew. I pushed her and dived for the hall. She fired and missed me as she fell against the bed.

I went down the stairs three at a time and hit the bottom one when the second shot came. At first I thought she had missed again. I was still running, and I felt nothing. Then, as I hit the door to the garden, I felt it. It was a slight itch in my back. My shoulder was suddenly numb. I tried to reach for the door with my right hand, but it wouldn't move. I had taken a bullet somewhere in the back, and I was scared as hell.

Behind me I could hear Brenda Beaumont padding down the stairs. I opened the door with my left hand and ran into the darkness near the pool.

Behind a row of trees I looked back and saw her perfect outline against the light from the house. She was looking frantically around. Then we both had the same idea. She started toward the barking dogs in the pool house. She was going to let them out to finish me. I ran along the trees about even with her, as she hurried toward the pool house.

She heard me and took another shot in my direction. The time she took gave me a few steps on her. I kept running. As I hit the back gate, I could hear her opening the front door of the pool house and Jamie and Ralph streaking for my scent.

I fumbled at the gate with my left hand and slammed it behind me as the dogs turned the corner. They leaped at the fence, but I was outside. I could see the blood seeping through my new jacket.

The light went on in the pool house, and the back door opened. Brenda Beaumont took another shot at me, but she was in panic now. One of the dogs whined pitifully and went down. The other dog stopped barking and turned curiously toward the fallen partner.

I didn't wait for her to take another shot. She might eliminate all of her watchdogs, but she also might hit me again. Dogs began barking and wailing all over. I ran as fast as I could into the trees.

The numbness was spreading as I ran. I was losing blood fast, but I had to make a call to Flynn. If I didn't make the call, there might not be an Errol Flynn by morning.

I managed to stumble into a street, but I stayed in the dark in case Brenda had wandered out after me. Her story was still good. Blackmailer shot.

The world was going dark, and I had visions of the inkwell. Taking a swim in it seemed a good idea, very comforting. I stumbled along to an intersection. I was heading for a house with a light on when I fell in the street. Somehow I had to get up and get to a phone, but I couldn't.

The car came around a curve, and I could see its lights coming toward me. The grill was a great chrome grin. My eyes closed, and I heard a screech of brakes. Then as I plunged into the inkwell for cover, I heard a car door slam in deep water. Koko the Clown greeted me and took my hand. I told him I had to get to a phone, but he paid no attention.

Koko led me to a drawing board the size of The Brown Derby. Brenda Beaumont stood looking at the board; Lynn Beaumont had her back turned. A huge hand came down from the sky and drew a cartoon of Cunningham on the board. Brenda stepped forward with an eraser and rubbed out the cartoon of Cunningham. Koko winked, and the huge hand came down and drew a cartoon of Harry Beaumont sneering. Brenda stepped forward and erased it. The huge hand came down a third time and drew a cartoon of me. I became the cartoon figure and saw Brenda walking toward me with the eraser. I looked up and pleaded with the cartoonist to let me go. He said he couldn't help me. I had been created to amuse Brenda and Lynn. But Lynn's back was still turned. Brenda stood in front of me, and I tried to turn and run into the picture. I felt the eraser touch my right shoulder, and the world went blank and white.

13

THE WORLD WAS WHITE, with a thin crack in it. The crack twisted to a corner, and my eyes followed it. I discovered that the world was a hospital room and I was in bed.

My brother stood next to the bed, his hands folded in front of him. He was looking down at me. His tie was back on, and his shirt was fresh. Seidman stood next to him.

I tried to say something, but my mouth was so dry nothing came out. Phil poured a glass of water from a pitcher on the table next to me. He handed the glass to me and I tried to reach out with my right hand. Nothing happened. I panicked and touched my right arm with my left hand to be sure it was there.

"It'll be all right," Seidman said dryly. "They fished a bullet out of your back. Another two inches, and it would have hit your heart."

"Lucky," I croaked.

"Maybe not," said Phil emotionlessly. "Who shot you?"

"I don't know," I said, trying to sit up. "It was dark and I was walking down the street minding my own business."

My idea was to keep Lynn Beaumont out of this if possible and let her have a mother. A father dead and a mother in jail in one day would be more than she deserved, and I knew something that was going to make it even harder on her. Brenda Beaumont hadn't killed anyone. She had just done some stupid things to protect her daughter. Since most of the stupid things had been done to me, I figured it was my business.

"You don't know who shot you?" Phil shook his head. He was beyond being angry with me. We were going through the motions. Seidman's little book was out, and he was taking notes again.

"Phil," I said, "what time is it?"

"Time for you to start leveling with me, Toby. You are in trouble." The lack of anger in his words was getting to me, but I needed information. "What time is it?"

"A few minutes after eleven," Seidman said, "but you're not going anywhere."

"Look," I said getting on my elbow, "I have to get to a phone. Someone is going to die unless I make a phone call."

"Who's going to die?" The question was Phil's.

"Errol Flynn."

Phil looked at Seidman in exasperation.

"Why is someone trying to kill Errol Flynn?" Phil asked.

"It's a little complicated," I said.

"Sure," Phil jumped in. "We'll try to understand. Meanwhile you explain why you killed Harry Beaumont."

"I didn't kill him."

"You want to try self defense?" Phil seemed to be making a serious suggestion.

"Look," I said, "I didn't kill Beaumont or Cunningham or whatever his name was and . . ."

"Deitsch, but you did throw a lamp at Delamater, who went for a one-way flight out of your window," Seidman pitched in. "You've been piling up too many corpses for a coincidence."

I tried again.

"Errol Flynn is going to be killed some time after midnight if you don't let me call him."

"O.K., you want to call Errol Flynn and save his life. Why don't you just give us the number, and we'll call him with your message and save his life. We'll give you all the credit." Phil was acting tough and sure, but he knew there was a chance of my telling the truth.

"Call the Beverly Wilshire, and ask for Rafael Sabatini in Room 1504," I said.

Phil exploded.

"Very funny, you two-bit piece of shit. You buy a certificate and a piece of tin, and you own the world. Well, I'm here to tell you that, brother or no brother, you're getting nailed for this and you deserve it. Tell him." His face was red as he turned away and moved to the window.

"You are under arrest for the murder of Harry Beaumont," Seidman said. "We're warning you that anything you say can be taken down by me and used in evidence against you."

I pointed a finger at Phil's back.

"You self-righteous bastard," I croaked, my voice cracking. "A man might die tonight because you think I'm playing games with you."

A frail man in white with blond hair and glasses came in. He looked young enough to be refused a drink in the worst dive in Pasadena.

"What's going on in here?" His voice was soprano. "I'm Doctor Parry, and I didn't operate on this man to have him die of shock brought on by you two."

"This man may be a murderer," said Seidman. Phil kept his back turned.

"He's a patient," said Young Doctor Parry, "my patient. I want both of you out of here, now."

"Look, doc," Phil said, turning menacingly. It was a good look, designed to wilt Dillinger, but it had no effect on Parry.

"You have thirty seconds to leave this room." Parry's voice was even. "If you haven't gone, I will file an official report stating that your presence here was a danger to my patient."

Seidman put his notebook away. Phil and Parry stared at each other for a few seconds, and then Phil moved to the door.

"A uniformed officer is going to spend the night outside this door," Phil said to Parry. "We'll be back tomorrow."

"Phil," I tried once more, "Call Flynn, believe me. Tell him to get out of that hotel room. Tell him . . ."

My brother slammed the door and left.

"You're not as sick as I told them," said Parry, adjusting his glasses and walking over to me. He turned me over and examined the bandage.

"Thanks, doc," I said.

"It wasn't for you," he said, turning me on my back again. "This is a hospital, not a police station."

"Doc, you've got to make a phone call for me."

"Not a chance, Mr. Peters. No breaks for them and none for you. That policeman said you might be a murderer."

"I'm not. I . . ."

"Forget it. I'll take care of your health. You take care of your personal problems."

He went out. It was up to me. I sat up, almost falling on the first try. The nausea passed, but the dizziness stayed with me. I didn't know how much blood I'd lost, but it was enough to make it tough for me to walk to the door.

I pushed the door open a crack. A big uniformed cop was sitting in a chair against the wall, looking at my door. He didn't look terribly bright, but he was doing his job.

My clothes were in the closet, at least my pants and shoes were. The jacket and shirt must have been too full of blood to save. Getting my pants on left-handed was the toughest part. I tucked the hospital nightgown in, hoping it might fool a nearsighted lunatic into thinking it was a shirt. The shoes went on without much trouble, but I couldn't tie them.

The big problem was wrapping the blankets up. I tore strips of sheet as quietly as possible. In about ten minutes, I had fashioned an unreasonable facsimile of a human dummy. It wouldn't have fooled anyone within twenty feet of it, but I looked out the window, and the ground was five stories below. As quietly as I could with one hand, I raised the window. Below me was a courtyard. No one was in it. I dropped the dummy out the window. Faint light from the windows of rooms gave it a sickly human look as it fell. I took the water glass and moved to the bathroom door. I threw the glass at the wall and let out as wild a yell as I could into my cupped hands. Then I ducked behind the door of the bathroom.

I heard the cop come running in. Through the crack in the bathroom door I saw him rush to the window and lean out.

His face was white when he turned, and I thought he was going to throw up. If he decided to do it in the bathroom, I was dead. Instead, he pulled himself together and went running out of the door. In a minute or less, he would know there was a dummy in the courtyard, and a dummy in a Los Angeles police uniform looking at it. Before he knew that, I had to be on my way.

There was still no feeling in my right arm and very little in my legs, but I made them work. They got me to the hall. A nurse was hurrying in my direction, her mouth open.

"He went out the window," I said, holding my face in my hands. She ran into my room.

There was an exit door in front of me, but it was sure to be the one the cop took. He wouldn't go for the elevator. At least that was the gamble I took. I went looking for the elevator and found it around a corner. Luck was with me. The elevator was on the floor.

The old man didn't even look at me as if I were dressed funny. He just took me down to the lobby.

About a dozen people were waiting there. I went past the desk.

"Please return your visitor's pass," a voice called to me, but I didn't stop. There was a coat rack in the corner of the lobby. I moved to it and grabbed a plaid jacket that looked as if it might fit me. If the owner were looking, I'd probably lose the use of my left arm, but I was on my way out the door.

A Red Top cab was waiting at the curb. I climbed in and said, "I'm Doctor Gillespie. There's an emergency, get moving."

It was a stupid thing to say, but the driver nodded seriously and pulled away. I turned around, and when we were half a block away, I could see the big cop standing at the curb looking both ways and seeing nothing.

There were two dimes in the coat of the jacket. I told the cabbie to stop at a drug store, and I ran in to call Flynn. It was 11:30 and time was running out.

There was no answer at Flynn's room. I had one dime left. Flynn might be in the hall or out for a sandwich. Either I went to the hotel and tried to get him out of there, or I went for the murderer and tried to keep him from getting to Flynn. I went back to the cab.

"How fast can you get me to Warner Brothers?"

"About ten minutes if I run a few lights." The cabbie was a moon-faced, fat guy with freckles.

"How about the Beverly Wilshire," I tried.

"You got emergencies at both places?" He was totally bewildered.

"Right," I said seriously.

"Maybe about the same time to get to Beverly Wilshire, but maybe less. The traffic's tough on the strip and . . ."

"Warner's, and fast," I said.

The L.A. speed limit was 25 for business and residential areas. We hit 60. He ran a few lights, but no sirens followed. At one point I thought I heard him chuckle with joy.

"Who's sick at Warner's?" he said, "Some star?"

"Who's your favorite star?"

"Cagney," he said. "Saw him last night at the Warner Theater downtown. You know how many times he's played a cabbie?"

"No," I said. The cab turned a corner and threw me against the door.

"Lots," said the chubby cab driver. "Is he hurt?"

"Yes," I said. "I've got to get there for an emergency operation."

"Shit," said the cabbie, and we jumped ahead. He was going to be part of saving Jimmy Cagney, friend to the cabbie.

"Pull right up to the gate," I said, as we shot down the street. He did.

"I'm Doctor Gillespie," I told the guard at the gate. "I just got a call. James Cagney has been injured."

The guard was a lot sharper than the cabbie.

"Cagney went home hours ago," he said.

"I don't care," I shouted. "He must have come back through the other gate. Now do you want to be responsible for serious injury to James Cagney?"

"I'll have to call," the guard said. "No one told me about this." He looked at me and the fat cab driver suspiciously and moved for the phone.

"That man is endangering the life of James Cagney," I said angrily to the cab driver. "I've got to get to my patient. Stop that guard if he tries to interfere."

The cab driver was confused, but he got out of the cab. I got out on the other side and moved into the lot.

"Hey, wait," shouted the guard, dropping the phone and taking a step toward me. He was an average-sized guy. The cabbie was a head shorter, about Cagney's height and eighty pounds heavier than his favorite actor. The cabbie got a bear hug on the guard.

I turned a corner as soon as I could. Behind me I could hear the guard shouting at the cabbie:

"What the hell are you doing, you goddamn nut!"

My killer was on this lot, and I had about fifteen minutes to find him before he made his way to Flynn. On a good day, in top condition, I could have made the rounds of all the buildings in half an hour, running at top speed. I had come close to it a few times when I worked at the studio.

Knowing the studio was the only edge I had. I knew about where to find my killer, but I was weak and getting weaker. I had to lean against a building and think. Even if I found him I wasn't sure what I could do in my condition, but a few ideas were coming.

The studio was dark except for the night lights. Some of the offices and editing rooms had lights on, but at a few minutes to midnight, it was nothing like it had been at noon.

My head cleared, and I tried to figure the route, to make it as easy on myself as I could. I tried five buildings and a few stages.

I struck it rich—or poor—in ten minutes. There was a light on in the stage where I had talked to Edward G. Robinson and Peter Lorre. It was the same light I had followed when I met Lorre, and he gave me the suggestion that had proved to be right.

Slowly and quietly I moved over and through the equipment and darkness to the office of Spade and Archer. There was a light on in the set, a single small light, but enough for me to see Spade's desk.

There was a man at the desk opening a drawer. As silently as I could, I moved to the sofa in Spade's office and sat, just as I was about to collapse. The man at the desk was so busy that he didn't hear me.

He was my killer and I greeted him. We were old friends.

"Hello, Hatch," I said softly.

14

HATCH JUMPED ABOUT A FOOT.

"Toby, what are you doing here?" His voice was friendly, but he knew something was in the air.

"I used to run the midnight check," I said. "I had a pretty good idea of what your route would be. I wanted to catch you before you went off duty."

Hatch stood up, his bulk blocking out the light behind him. He was a dark mass in front of me. I thought about my friendly inkwell, but I fought it off.

"Why did you want to catch me?" he said. "Mr. Adelman told me about Mr. Flynn. I was going to head there as soon as I finished. He'd be . . ."

"Dead within ten minutes of your getting to him," I said.

"Dead? Mr. Flynn? Me?"

He took a step toward me.

"Right. You want to go over the whole thing, Hatch, so we can decide what we're going to tell the cops, or do you go on screwing things up."

He stood over me. I still couldn't see his face, but I could bet he was holding onto the friendly uncle grin.

"Toby, you look sick. Let me get you to a doctor."

He reached a big arm down to me, and I could feel his fingers dig into my remaining good shoulder.

"Forget it, Hatch, it's all over." I twisted away from him. "Brenda tried to kill me tonight. She missed. She's not as good a shot as you, but then you were shooting at men at close range, except for Flynn, and you missed him."

"Toby . . ."

"Shit, Hatch, I knew as soon as I saw the photograph in Brenda's room, the family photograph. You're Harry Beaumont's old man, and Lynn is your granddaughter."

"Well, yes," he stammered, "but . . ."

"But you killed your own son." I had to keep him off balance. Maybe I could get him as weak emotionally as I was physically.

Hatch gave in. He moved back to the desk and sat. His big hand went to his face and pushed his guard's cap back. The light was still behind him. His voice sounded as if he might be sobbing.

"He deserved it, Toby, believe me, he deserved it. He was going to use that negative, his own daughter . . ."

"Take it from the beginning, Hatch," I said. "All I have is a rough cut. You give me the final edit."

His body heaved like a great whale, and he talked softly, moving from anger to tears:

"Harry got me this job years ago when he started to move up, but he didn't want anyone to know I was his father. He was right. Everything was fine. I'd visit the family. I love that girl, Toby. Lynn is a wonderful girl."

"Well, when Harry saw that picture of Flynn and my granddaughter, he came to me and told me about it, told me about the exchange for the negative."

"I was waiting for you when you got there. I walked in behind you. Cunningham recognized me. I had seen him plenty of times at the gate. I had to hit you, to get the negative and the picture. I didn't want to kill you."

I let that pass. There were a few things he was going to juggle, but they weren't important. He sure as hell had tried to kill me when he shot his son.

"I hit you," Hatch continued, "and then grabbed Cunningham and took the negative. He found your gun on the floor where it fell. I grabbed it from him and shot him. I wasn't sorry.

"I brought the gun, the money, the negative and the print you had to Harry. He said I'd been stupid, and he took them; but I had a good look at the negative."

"You believed it," I helped him. "That's why you took a shot at Flynn the next morning. Hatch, for all the good it will do you, Lynn was never with Errol Flynn or anyone else. The picture was a fake."

The sob was clear and real.

"No need to lie to me, Toby. It's too late."

"No lie, Hatch. Why didn't you just ask the girl? She would have told you."

He stood up angrily.

"How could I ask her a thing like that? I love that girl."

"What about the boys who came to get the piece of picture from me?" I went on, trying to keep him talking.

"That was Brenda's idea. I told her about Delamater. I didn't like it, but . . ."

"And your son?"

"Harry," he sighed. "Harry tried to blackmail both Brenda and the studio with the negative. After she left the house yesterday, she called me. When he came on the lot this morning, I tried to talk to him, to get the negative, but he wouldn't give it.

"Then, when you came I trailed behind you. I saw you fighting. I followed you to the Rockne set . . ."

"Took a shot at me, killed Harry and took the negative and the money," I finished. "Where are they now?"

"I couldn't get off the lot," Hatch continued, wiping sweat from his bald head, "so I hid them in this desk in a prop along with your gun. I knew the set wouldn't be used for a while."

Hatch walked around to the other side of the desk and opened the bottom drawer. He lifted out the figure of a black bird and from its hollow base he pulled out a small brown envelope. He put the bird on the desk where it stared at me while I stared at Hatch who now had my gun in his hand.

"That's my gun, Hatch. I'd like it back." I didn't think I had enough strength left to take it from him even if he handed it to me.

"Sorry, Toby. If you talk, then everyone finds out about Lynn. I don't care about myself so much, but that girl . . . ."

"Bull *shit,*" I said, with as much strength as I could pull together. "Both you and Brenda are doing it all for Lynn. Why didn't you try asking her what she wanted before the two of you went around killing people and . . . What's the use? You've messed this up so badly I don't see how you can keep her name out of it."

He tore up the negative.

"Not enough," I said, "but I'll make a deal. Turn yourself in, confess, make up some story about kidnapping or something, and we can keep Lynn out of it. You can work out the story with a lawyer. Brenda has enough money to get you a good one. Do that, and I throw in an extra: I forget Brenda tried to kill me. That way Lynn keeps her mother. She's lost her father, who wasn't worth much, and is sure as hell going to lose her grandfather."

He held up his hand to stop me from talking.

"Sorry, Toby."

The gun came up and aimed for my chest. I thought about leaping into the darkness, and I might have made it that far, but I didn't have the strength to crawl away after that. He'd just walk over and shoot me.

"Don't be a sap, Hatch. With me gone, there's no one to blame the killings on. The cops will find you."

The gun leveled. I had been beaten, screwed, shoved in a closet and shot in the back by various members of the Beaumont family. Now one of them was going to kill me, and I was still trying to help them. Maybe my brother was right.

Then I heard a sound. It was inside the building but far away, a kind of squeak and swish. Hatch didn't hear it. He took a step toward me to make sure he didn't miss.

In the light behind Hatch, I could see something moving quickly from the ceiling. It got bigger and in my woozy state, it seemed to be moving in slow motion.

It was a man swinging down behind Hatch on an equipment

rope. The man was Errol Flynn, in a billowy white shirt. I made the leap into darkness as Hatch fired and missed and turned to watch as Flynn's flying feet hit him squarely in the back.

Hatch lumbered forward hitting the sofa I had just been sitting in. My gun flew, and Flynn dropped neatly to the ground.

"I've always wanted to do that," he said brightly.

Hatch made a lunge for him, but Flynn was too fast. The actor moved to the side and threw a fist to Hatch's head. The big man went down in a heap.

"Please don't get up again, old man," Flynn said sincerely. "I really don't enjoy hitting you."

Flynn picked up my gun and moved to my side to help me up. He handed me the gun. I managed to hold onto it and aim it at Hatch, who struggled to his feet.

"Heard the whole thing," Flynn said shaking his head. "Hatch, Toby told you the truth. I never saw your granddaughter before yesterday."

"Errol," I said, "you heard the deal I offered Hatch. Is it all right with you if it stays open?"

Hatch looked hopefully at Flynn.

"Of course. It also keeps my name out of this and the studio happy."

"Thanks," said Hatch.

I asked Flynn to take the money and leave the torn negative in Spade and Archer's wastebasket. He supported me with one hand, and Hatch walked in front of us.

"What were you doing here?" I asked Flynn.

"Ironic, my friend, truly ironic," he replied. "Fate is a wondrous thing. As I told you, I had decided that I had had enough of hiding. I would not spend another night cowering in that hotel. I came here to tell Hatch not to bother to stand bodyguard duty. I came in just as you chastised him for a few murders. Then I got the brilliant idea of using the rope. I shall always remember that moment, savor it, actually."

"You saved my life," I said.

"Yes, I did, didn't I?" His grin was broad.

Hatch made the call from a phone in Flynn's dressing room. I gave him my brother's number. Flynn got on the phone and suggested that they also send an ambulance for me.

My brother must have asked who was talking because Flynn said:

"Errol Flynn. I'm an actor."

Flynn poured himself a drink, and one for Hatch, who took it. I declined. We let Hatch call Brenda and arrange for a lawyer to meet him at the station.

Our march to the gate was a ridiculous sight. Flynn half carried me, and Hatch marched glumly in front of us.

Just before we reached the gate a big black car stopped next to us, and a little man jumped out. His hair, what there was of it, was black. So was his suit.

"Flynn," said Jack Warner, "is that man drunk?" He pointed at me.

"No, Mr. Warner, he's sick."

Warner gave Flynn an unbelieving look, sure that he was being made the butt of a silly practical joke involving Flynn and one of his drunken friends.

"Does he work for me?" Warner asked.

"Not exactly," Flynn replied.

"Good," said Warner, getting back in his car. "Then get him off the lot."

That was exactly what he had said four years ago when he fired me.

I let out a laugh and slumped against Flynn. Warner gave me a last look and a shake of his head and pulled away.

I passed out and woke up four days later.

15

THE DAY I GOT OUT OF THE HOSPITAL, the first thing I did was call my sister-in-law to find out how my nephew was. She said he was fine. I didn't talk to my brother.

Flynn had paid my hospital bills. Part of the expenses, he said. He also paid me my fee for every day I was in the hospital. I took it.

With towing, taxi fares, parking, ruined clothes, phone calls and broken window thrown in, the fee was $464.90.

Hatch had confessed. The story he concocted was part self-defense and part insanity. It was so confused and complicated that it might convince a jury. He had kept out all mention of Lynn, Flynn, me and Warner Brothers.

My arm was still in a sling. I had a steak at Al Levy's Tavern on Vine and took a Yellow cab to the studio. Sid Adelman was expecting me.

Esther was still reading her magazine, and F.D.R. was still on the desk. The Warner boys were on the wall, and a new writer had moved into Bill Faulkner's office.

"What happened to Faulkner?" I said.

"Didn't work out," Sid answered. "What can I do for you?"

"You got your $5,000 back, and the negative was destroyed. You owe me two hundred bucks."

He got up and moved for the refrigerator.

"You want a beer?"

"No," I said, "I want two hundred bucks. You were willing to pay thousands for that picture, and I got rid of it for you. Now you're arguing about a lousy few hundred bucks."

Sid straightened his jacket and nodded, always the man to accept a good argument.

"You're a schmuck," he said, pulling out his wallet and handing me two hundred dollar bills, "but I always said you were honest. You want your job back here?"

"No thanks," I said. "Mr. Warner and I don't get along."

"You're not the only one," he said, "but that doesn't keep them from working here and getting rich."

I pocketed the money and started for the door when the phone rang. Sid answered and caught me as I touched the knob.

"For you," he said.

I took it. A woman's voice, frightened, musical and familiar answered.

"Mr. Peters," she said. "Thank goodness I found you. I called your office, and Dr. Minck said I could reach you there. Errol Flynn said you might be able to help me. I need help."

"Who is this?" I said, reaching for a pencil on Sid's desk, "and where can I meet you?"

"My name is Judy Garland, and you can meet me at M.G.M as quickly as you can get here. Please hurry, Mr. Peters. I . . ."

Something or someone cut her off in mid-sentence. I ran for the door, without saying goodby to Sid Adelman or Warner Brothers.

THE TOBY PETERS MYSTERIES

FROM MYSTERIOUSPRESS.COM
AND OPEN ROAD MEDIA

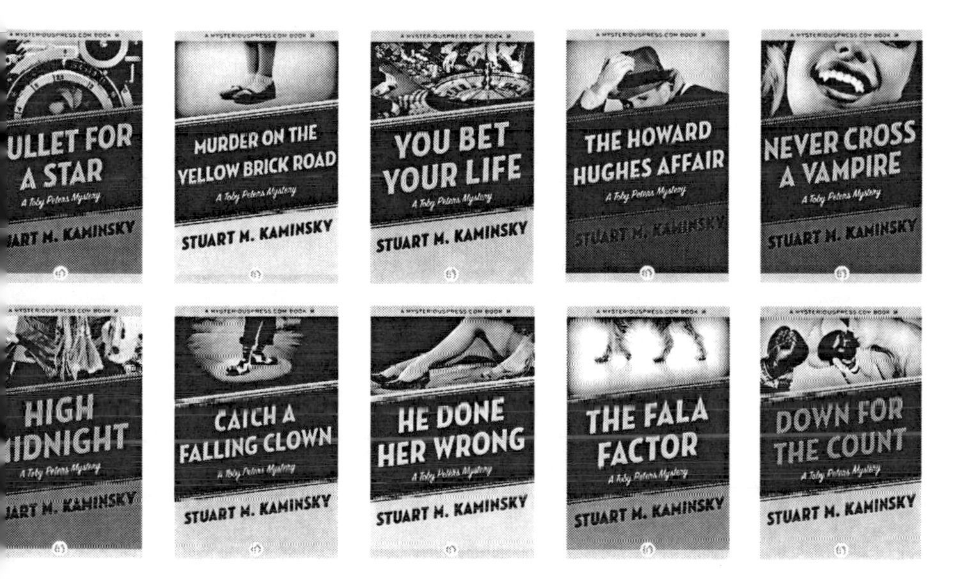

Available wherever ebooks are sold

MYSTERIOUSPRESS.COM

OPEN ROAD
INTEGRATED MEDIA

CPSIA information can be obtained at www.ICGtesting.com
Printed in the USA
LVOW07s1809150515

438698LV00004B/107/P